Weaving the Tapestry of Life

A Book of Poetry
by James R. Ellerston

Published 2019, by James R. Ellerston Pella, IA 50219 USA

A.A. of the Tryon Arts and Crafts School
(Agnes Matteson Sternberg)

Throughout her days she spread golden threads of family love,
wove a fabric of wholesome living from the spinning wheel of life,
made her art from the practical cloth of daily events,
spread a welcoming table for nurturing meals for family and friends,
served with pleasure to the children of her world.

Entering life on the windswept plains of Saskatchewan,
fathered by a man homesteading the Canadian prairie for grain,
raising her, a younger sister, and a brother a few miles from town;
after one hundred years of life (she survived cancer twice); she died
in the mountains of North Carolina-- amongst blue ridged valleys.

Crafted spokes of her ticking clock of earthly time have stopped,
 her unused yarns no longer await the magic of her weaving loom;
days of craftsmanship with warp and shuttle passed on to pupils;
the last of a generation has now left the family behind
and returned to fertile-tended earth in her eternal garden.

James R. Ellerston
September 28, 2018

Weaving the Tapestry of Life

A.A. of the Tryon Arts and Crafts School (September 28, 2018)

September 2017
I Awake So Early

October 2017
The Windmill Turns Counting Hours this Darkening Day

November 2017
Breathe on Me, Breath of God
"Comfort Ye"; the Search to Soothe

December 2017
Time Capsule
("All I Want for Christmas is")
      This Gift of Modern Medicine and God
F.D Artist Gone (Jeremy Dylan Cladeira)
My Wish: A Poem Could Fix It For My Boy

January 2018
A Boy's Cars
Before the Ballpoint; Writing Instrument
Parents' Hopefulness
After the Iceman Cometh

February 2018
Pella Opera House: Seven Minutes to Closing
Weather Reports for Previous Days
No Penalty Box for Violations of Rules in a Deadly Game
I Can't Sing Without Thinking
Lucy in a Photo
Colorado Youth Fights to Place in Life
Unwanted Side Effects Cause Social Problems
Only Their Buried Art Survived the Gassings
For Billy
Central To Their Future Hope

March 2018

Applaud Voting With One's Feet

The Cost of Knowledge

The Clock Stopped, Love Went On

Keeping the Faith After the Classroom Bell Rings

Wordless Poetry and Verse Loving Daily

Arms Are For Hugging

April 2018

2018 "Superstar" at Near Fifty Years

Central Women's Chorus 2018 Debut

Flashing Evening Lights

A Mobile Army Surgical Hospital:

      MASH: Much About Soldiers' Honor

Diplomacy Set to Music

May 2018

City Tulip Festival Disrupted

Only in Pella

Saturday Spent With Family Friend

William Penn University Commencement 2018

Slice of Life (Children in Wartime)

Visit to Kuyper House: Memory of 1966

Christian Riley Garcia R.I.P. May 18, 2018

      Sante Fe, Texas High School Hero

My Read in Church Prayer Created Controversy

June 2018

Tuned Into the World

First Aid Kit, Saving Souls

Satisfying Garden Salad

In Green Pastures

In Remembrance of Me

Legacy

Thankful Time for Days' End Rest

Homecoming 2018
After the Summer of '68
Woodbine Willie (Geoffrey Studdert Kennedy)

October 2018
Last Car Ride (from a photo Jessica posted)
Sheila's Horses (in Photographs)
dawn celebrated
Easter Sunday Dinner After Church
Prayer for Another Baby
House Saving Mechanicals
Encourage Another on Their Journey
Desire to Communicate with Horses
October 7th, 2011
Poetry from the Press: Immigration Inquiry
Absolution? A Solution
For Former Student Mike Tuvell
For Students: History Writing Must be Verified Again
Still Considering Matthew Shepard After Twenty Years
Fortune Cookie Truth
Revised Recipe for Dylan's Dairy Restaurant:
                Mix Love, Cancer, A Herd of Milk Cows
Song and Dance In a Gym
Bridge Over Troubled Waters
October 26, 2018: It Will Come To Pass
Few Rivers Flow North (Song for the Caravan)
Guardian Angels Driving Lanes Among Us
75th Anniversary "Oklahoma Hello"
Getting The Ashes Home
Disguised Hatred is So Political
Alex Craig: Cheerleader for Ending Conflict

I Awake So Early

to see gray fog in pre-dawn light
obscuring shore and tree line far;
distant watery surface blended with sky;
dark shadows stretch out lines of western views.

it is a quiet morning without song of loon or gull;
coffee warms my mug cupped in elderly hands;
dog and wife still slumber securely,
missing solitude in spinning clouds.

hesitation blankets lake's early morning sleep;
sun bright beacons come up, the swirling curtains lift,
and the day begins to play out its drama, with the duet
paddling the canoe across the wet and rippling stage of blue.

James R. Ellerston
September 7, 2017

The Windmill Turns Counting Hours this Darkening Day

Autumn breezes blow leaves and spin blades,
the unsailed windmill turns, counting days
towards winter's gales
in the bustling corner of the village.

Temperatures drop and people hurry as they walk,
postal counters line up with packages,
coffee sales increase in the corner shop;
no longer summer sun but fall days.

Do not cloud person's future hopes,
despite the world news,
which does not hinder smiles from faces
and silent greetings amongst the optimistic.

Without fallen cheeks and downcast eyes
we struggle and shuffle along life's patterns;
carved pumpkin dentures and ghoulish costumes
help us through this ever darkening day.

Evening is about restoring glee to jovial youth,
whose outstretched hands in our lands of plenty
seek generosity from strangers' lit up homes
and sweet treats and gifts in bags and baskets.

In lands of need and poverty there is a different story,
while distended bellies cry for milk in lands of famine
without the luxury of cable news and crazed drivers of trucks
using a vehicle as a scythe in the late afternoon on a street.

But we are given hope from Mary's small hut in Scotland,
where it has been proven done with fundraising efficiency;
a billion charitable meals have been cooked and flowed forth
to reach the world's starving young at village schools.

Feed innocent souls and minds as days shorten, hopes descend;
give a reason to believe missiles will not rain down;
from countries that would let hungry children starve
or mow down those in the way-- such painful news on cell phones.

James R. Ellerston   October 31, 2017

Breathe on Me, Breath of God

the young minister stood there in his khaki pants
and bright blue shirt,
but when he announced the death of the young man
in this idyllic community so unexpected at age 13,
(from asthma on the Thursday before)
the pastor's voice cracked emotionally in the pulpit,
and the congregation within this comforting sanctuary
struggled to inhale the reality of the Lord's mercy.

when the minister left the platform
and sat in the vacant seat at the end of the pew,
he was with the grieving young man
who was hearing "Why?" screaming in his head;
and the voice sat there next to him praying
in communion with those together, invoking
His presence to fill the church this Sunday morning.

the young church goer mourning in his seat
felt comfortable wiping his eyes
over and over again
amongst us all;
and I was not able to sing the choir music in front of me,
my eyes moist, voice silent.

after church in the Walmart
I heard a young teenage boy telling his parents,
"I didn't know how much I loved him";
two mothers in the aisle looked each other deeply in the eye
and whispered quietly;
there were 120 photos of Caiden Christopher Knox,
posted on the internet obituary this Sunday afternoon;
I wept today over a beautiful child of God now gone;
someone I never met and didn't know about
until today in church when led in prayer from a pew.

James R. Ellerston
November 12, 2017

"Comfort Ye"; the Search to Soothe

The two of you sat right in front of me, hands wringing,
at the funeral for the beautiful middle-school student
who had run out of the breath of life--
 in a hospital after an asthma attack;
the death of the thirteen year-old boy
causing a community of adults and children to mourn, question, pray.

The two of you sat right in front of me, hands folded,
your anguished mother seeking out a way to help you through it,
to aid your understanding and questioning being,
your grieving face betraying distress to your parent in every deep glance
your eyes looking into her tissue-wiped eyes
as she searched to soothe your grown-up pain over and over again.

The two of you sat right in front of me, hands clasped;
her hand in the center of your young man's back
touching you in another time as a mother and her child,
trying to sooth the ingestion of a hard life fact,
hoping for a burp after a gasping infant meal;
giving reassurance that there was still love in this place, this world.

The two of you sat right in front of me, hands clenched in belief
as your yet-unshaven face found again the moistened eyes,
her wadded Kleenex wiping repeatedly;
I never saw her face, only his;
I am unsure whether he was looking into her face searching for an answer,
or comforting her in her pain for him.

I am writing now, grieving at this later time after that Tuesday they sat in front of me,
but still feeling guilty even observing these tender moments between parent and child;
we were all sitting in a church building full of young people swaddled in arms of love;
parents, children, and believers confronting the reality that only life on earth is finite!
it was a gray cold day with a biting breeze, clouded skies weeping tears, while
across from the church middle-schoolers held blue balloons to release heavenward.

James R. Ellerston
November 18, 2017

Time Capsule

after 37 years Voyage 1 has fired up its trajectory thrusters
manufactured by Aerojet Rocketdyne,
still ready after 4 decades of dormancy.

where is it now, this vessel of adventurying man?
carrying mankind's hopes and dreams,
to voyage amongst the starry night.

the spacecraft and lovers' eyes
doth travel together through space and time of 37 years, where
thrusters direct the wishes of scientists across interstellar distance.

19 hours and 35 minutes each way for the communications,
but a verified use extends the usable life by 2 or 3 more years,
by using guidance engines last used in 1986.

James R. Ellerston
December 1, 2017

("All I Want for Christmas is")
This Gift of Modern Medicine and God

Conceived in vitro with love and science,
tonight this fragile embryo of parental longing
will spend its first sheltered night
in the comforting warmth of my daughter's womb.

Today carefully removed from a harsh cold freezer
after preservation in time suspending storage,
it was so quickly implanted today in a uterine home now
ready and welcomed to reside for months of growth.

Wishes from loving family fly forth to end anguished hope,
traveling miles from distant states and loyal friends;
this mere speck on an ultrasound image so very minute--
God's imagination now nourished by mother's love and blood.

James R. Ellerston
December 6, 2017

F.D. Artist Gone (Jeremy Dylan Cladeira)

Your medium was ink in skin,
the tapestry of trust and life;
people bare your work with selfless pride,
drawings that are now life-worn masterpieces,
surpassed only by the heavens' stars
now surrounded by clients' love.

I wrote this for you Ryan Crowl
James R. Ellerston
December 7, 2017

My Wish: A Poem Could Fix It For My Boy

Do not despair, my son whom I love eternally so,
more than ocean spray driven by relentless wind crashing distant shores,
more than the planetary worlds voyaging through orbiting time,
making arcs in space, spinning night into golden day with sunrise light.

Oh let me motion down with victorious swaths away
the hateful harshness of a darkening world.
from now breaking open heart and tender sight
with all living power to move your stumbling steps forward
in these hesitant days. power and arise you in morning's painful dawn
with energy to set the ugly and hateful right.

I worship your talented imparting of nurtured skill
sending practiced music to others' empty hollow spheres of being;
you impart art and beauty uplifting the burdened poor
upon their downtrodden laboring paths;
somehow live with the drive to exist all your earthbound days
with the energy the generous and all encompassing God allows you.

Drive out today others' hate and squalor, pain and sorrow;
keep up the fight please– to live in hope and hold better dreams
with mate and family, loyal friends, who will love you
and grip you firm and timeless through every black tomorrow;
remember they are hanging on and holding you tight,
never letting you go though mind has pain and muscles ache.

I love your grown self today with the same powerful emotion,
the same fervent love I changed each dirty diaper with delicate cleansing;
I would now continue to hope decent upstanding people
will drive out this painful current political shit
away from your irritated vulnerable cherished skin.

My love for you awakened me in the middle of the night,
December 11, 2017
James R. Ellerston

A BOY'S CARS

There is a reality in the mind of any grandchild
in a created field of carpet fiber made of trees and grass,
highways of imagination across the Great Plains
reaching across a playroom between
the black mountain of the grand piano
and the cliff of oak book shelves,
too high to climb on a chair.

Interstates of plastic pavement mold raceways
for push and release cars and trucks,
stretching fertile fields of thought
with what to do next.

There was always another singing truck or car to activate,
it's voice bursting forth in songs
for the animated soul of motor vehicles
driving a plastic world in child's hands.

A grandma sitting in this cluttered world of toys
talked in characters' voices in her Italian
making real the red Ferrari
brought from Italy in her suitcase,
as it powerfully drove within his miniature world,
with miles to go,
and tearful protest before bedtime sleep.

James R. Ellerston
January 10, 2018

Before the Ballpoint; Writing Instrument

my mother had a fountain pen
and wrote in beautiful cursive hand;
I looked upon her desk spread paper
as the golden point between a pianists fingers
flowed in skilled hand across the page.

with Schaeffer magic from a blue ink bottle
filling up the internal bladder
by having used the golden lever on the sided;
using luxury in a skilled executives hands,
built in Fort Madison with Iowa pride.

James R. Ellerston
January 11, 2018

Parents' Hopefulness

Repetitive sound of a heartbeat
from an embryo so small yet alive,
now living six weeks in a mother's womb--
visible only by technical equipment--
so small in an image of black, gray, and white;
but the regularity of the tiny internal pump
makes a signature delight in yearning minds
of parents and grandparents alike;
it is reminiscent of the pulse heard in a man's chest
when a woman's head listens in delight
upon the breath heaved muscles
of lungs at the start of peaceful nights.

James R. Ellerston
January 11, 2018

After the Iceman Cometh

The mailman cometh
is not the name of the famous play of social agony
by the famous playwright Eugene O'Neill,
but is my pet dog's morning ritual.

Starting at ten in the morning,
come rain or shine, snow or sleet,
even though the postman often does not cometh
until the early afternoon these wintry days.

To deliver our bills and greeting cards,
sometimes after sharp nails of paws have scratched window sills,
danced on hardwood floor beneath the sash,
and harsh barks of a song of greeting and alarm.

By delivery hours have passed with the anxious dog,
sunshine's warmth is streaming through
the big south window facing streetward,
a location of winter's heating sun.

We are awaiting packages on a concrete stoop
and the cessation of the infernal barking
when the letters and parcels are gathered in
to the eager sniffing nose within.

James R. Ellerston
January 17, 2018

Pella Opera House: Seven Minutes to Closing

spacious room, empty space, exhibit for humanity;
silence, bodies moving, no speaking, no sound,
a quiet, not even a shuffling of shoes;
people moving along the panels' pictures;
string music over speakers engaging sorrow.

persons looking, seeing intensely
where these few hid together
in a quiet so whispered
the toilet could sometimes not be flushed.

our wordless pain held in reserve
in an agonized body that shook our moistening eyes
as we left to our parked security
on our familiar hometown street.

a tender girl again looked out at me in photos,
some the familiar black and white poses
from decades of new editions;
(book jacket photos that sold this famous diary.)

here pictured in front of my retired teacher's struggling mind--
a whole classroom of young children with their instructor--
youth who never became adults, a lover, a parent;
all gone up the chimneys.

beautiful large color enlargements showed where they lived,
in fearful hiding in the Secret Annex;
a place where Anne Frank's diary lays again on her desk;
a red and white plaid birthday present to become a book
empowering words of love and hope once heard by the world.

James R. Ellerston
February 4, 2018

Weather Reports for Previous Days

alarming forecasts make us think of friends
in other cities on the weather maps
where of necessity people must make long commutes
or those whose slanted driveways could cause a body to fall.

looking out my 8 o'clock front window with my aggressive dog
we see uphill traffic backed-up on Hazel Street;
orange busses and cars climbing the slope to school
remind me of desperate cars spinning out decades earlier on Kenyon Road.

teachers had seen vehicles struggling out their classroom windows
for apprehensive hours previous to sensible early dismissal;
ignoring evenings shoveling snow, as children we celebrated white fluff;
as older adults we regret and fear the inches of falling flakes.

today those past streets are now four lanes
and front wheel drive cars climb the hospital hill easily;
thousands drive the daily commute to college classes
informed by atmospheric reports and guesses.

I cancelled my own weekend trip to see other friends
and over Facebook advised another not to travel home to family;
an east-west highway is snowbound across the state map;
your hometown reports a snowfall of eleven inches on the television news.

James R. Ellerston
February 9, 2018

No Penalty Box for Violations of Rules in a Deadly Game

while the decades of Korean DMZ truce still hold
there is a joint effort to play Olympic Games together;
athletes from two sides of a map line still technically at war
form one hockey team and take the ice as a unified effort,
to chase a puck as one nation and skate together.

God's gift of muscle, verve, athleticism, bravura
has enabled the seventeen-year-old youth on a snowboard,
from his upbringing in the snows of Colorado,
to be the youngest ever winning a golden medal in this daring sport
where being invincible in youth is necessary for repeated attempts in practice.

those who guide our American nation in international relations
have come to the Olympics playing games of whose hand to shake,
when to stand, when to sit, whom to be near in a line of world leaders,
which place is one assigned to sit at a banquet table;
the questions of the leaders who voice the policy of our diplomacy.

yet those who elsewhere wage this week their evil games of warfare
did not follow rules of Conventions or long held agreements from Geneva,
but in this week of reaching for international brotherhood
some have used banal toxic substances on Syrian civilians, children, babies;;
our lamentations cry out for the innocents.

for what U.N referees have called crimes against humanity,
no one has been put in a penalty box.

James R. Ellerston
February 11, 2018

I Can't Sing Without Thinking

in your college days, you may have wondered
why I was not singing standing with you
on such a familiar song we all know
this morning during church;
I will share this from my past.

our choir anthem as the sun shone again
on that Sunday after 9-11
was a powerful arrangement of Amazing Grace;
and I cannot sing it these many years later
without choking up and eyes moistening.

James R. Ellerston
February 11, 2018

Lucy in a Photo

it is funny how one falls in love
with other persons' dogs;
some visited at cabins or swimming in the lake,
others at invited dinners over holidays,
bounding the house until they come to our arms;
but the response is always the same
as adoring eyes gaze into a camera and our mind.

a picture comes up over Facebook daily
of the neighbor's dog long gone,
or a friends' pet still prancing the house,
or a dog one had seen summer after summer on a dock;
photographed with too-soon-grown children hugging and holding
these pets,
and like a child our hands' muscle memory reaches out,
still petting that tender soft fur of a still breathing beloved animal.

in our embracing hurried soul
when art shows no more than a daylight backlit photo,
but red-brown fur covers legs stretched out in morning's light,
a nose rests comfortable in pose on a black leather sofa--
a pet permitted on the leather upholstery for years of joy;
our hearts are swollen again at the sight of a posted picture
with those golden eyes and canine expression of trust
now felt across the passage of time
and miles of highway between us.

James R. Ellerston
February 12, 2018

Colorado Youth Fights to Place in Life

wearing carefully chosen white-rimmed canvas shoes
the young boxer danced within the ring of restaurant diners
learning the ropes of waiting midwest tables well
with closely choreographed foot moves providing service.

in the contest to keep a good job at age fourteen,
now he's clad in the basic work uniform of young manhood,
his blue denim jeans shout the athletic muscles of developed thigh and calf,
while adept biceps carry food laden platters.

there is only a short period of abundant choices growing up in life,
in the fight for winning blows and surviving best chances;
he could choose to wrestle his way to life's winning podium,
or run for a goal line ahead of others on the green field of success.

such gene-driven beauty in any maturing youthful adonis
attracts the eyes of seeking would-be high school suitors,
those between bells standing by steel lockers lining classroom hallways,
wishing for a Friday night date, to spend his Sunday night earnings.

this teen draws a fine line between conveying courtesy and over familiarity,
but is friendly meeting varied needs of evening customers' requests;
in a future sometime he might put a pen to paper and write his hidden thoughts,
encouraged to draw mountains of ideas from a past not as simple as it seems,

humor is hidden behind an attractive face and beneath beautiful strands of hair,
and a yet unbroken boxer's nose above a contagious smile;
fast-forward seventy successful grandchild-blessed years to a now aging man,
as he champions a walker in a tango down a long hall to elderly eating together.

James R. Ellerston
February 12, 2018

Unwanted Side Effects Cause Social Problems

It shouldn't be a question
of how many
but why any
since the new calendar year started.

People do or don't want to decide the counting
of the suicide of a teen
who kills himself in a high school restroom
as a school shooting; or is it a society failure?

Debates restart or continue
with old inquiries or rehashed justifications;
constitutional issues of life and staying alive should outweigh
issues of liberty and happiness for firearm purchases.

Mental health medication designers for adolescents
must realize the importance of functional body desires
to the troubled young males who pull automatic triggers
after putting their orgasm blocking pills in the trash.

Eliminating unwanted side-effects in antidepressants like Prozac
will increase functionality and attractiveness to struggling teens;
pharmacy solutions must surpass prescribing the least expensive
in favor of drugs preserving personality, creativity, and sexuality.

James R. Ellerston
February 16, 2018

Only Their Buried Art Survived the Gassings

It was only the buried art of Terezin that remained
from the Czech town that became a Camp;
a holding pen for Jewish children
allowed to draw and paint, and write their informed poems
which posthumously survived after the train rides East.

In a short hour on the theater stage
all was acted out before our breaking hearts
as our school youngsters of today portrayed these doomed youth;
we heard the ominous sound of SS boots marching in evil step,
saw students carry their one case to the rattling sounds of trains.

Our supper-table family was torn from its home,
away from a circle around the bread and candle before our eyes;
a scene where the terrified father admonishes his adolescent son
who in the cracking teen voice of an overly-brave young man
argues with optimism that they can't just give up.

Student art adorns a classroom wall, poems are read aloud;
young lovers are married an hour before their eastbound train;
Hebrew is cantored, English prayers are solemnly recited;
more baggage is marched across the staged street;
in the end only two were costumed; all else eternal in angels' white.

James R. Ellerston
February 17, 2018
the play "I Never Saw Another Butterfly" by Celeste Raspanti
Des Moines Young Artists' Theatre
Stoner Theater, Des Moines, Iowa

For Billy

It was the Book uplifted in the Hand,
delivering the Word to the World
with the Voice of a Call for Peace and Love,
once heard by World Leaders, Queen and Presidents,
Millions in tents, stadiums, and over the electronic airwaves
at the Pulpit on the Television,
Preaching to a Planet in need of His Message conveyed as Truth;
our spiritual Paths have crossed;
my Candle is lit for this beloved Man,
Rev. Graham.

James R. Ellerston
February 21, 2018

Central To Their Future Hopes

Watching the Theatre play Thursday night,
eighty-five minutes about the world's refugee population,
an unstoppable tap on the interrupted and ruined lives
flowing from the open faucets of warfare and subjugation.

People flooding a troubled planet between here and there
without the dedication of resources by affluent nations
to meet the basic human needs of these hopeful persons,
who have moved onward across borders from home and family.

Marching across deserts, mountains, political differences,
they are crossing the swollen waves of vicious seas,
some surviving the heartbreak when children lost and drowned
sink to watery graves from overloaded inadequate sunken boats.

A red-faced carrot-topped world leader speaks out against
ethnic and chain migration "bringing in the bad peoples";
while those of us dismayed at home in disbelief still want
to hold up the welcoming lamp beside an open golden door.

James R. Ellerston
February 22, 2018
ANON(ymous) by Naomi-Iizuka
Commissioned by The Children's Theatre Company, Minneapolis
Kruidenier Theatre February 21-24, 2018 Pella, Iowa

Applaud Voting With One's Feet

voting with his feet, step in front of step, escaping away;
give him a canteen, food, water;
don't lock him in a camp!

in the heat of the rising sun at four years old
wearing dusty pants he walks isolated alone
bravely trodding across the sand and clay flat desert before him,
a migration from Syria to Jordan by gazing at the distant horizon--
his compass-- his shadow on the ground guiding him in blazing sunshine
until the team of U.N. men caught up with him on his quest.

his dirty hand was clenching the handles of the plastic shopper tightly;
when tired he would sit and open the bag,
smell hot plastic and the scent of the garments of his mother and sister,
now corpses behind him but never to be forgotten.

family members were killed in Syria, now dead in his terrorized past,
their cherished clothes are all he has the strength to carry,
in little hands clutching onto their dream on his journey;
somehow he finds the courage to stand again and walk toward a new life.

hike on and on, mouth parched and belly aching
somehow he moves onward searching for a new home;
reporter/photographer Adran Yahya is feeling heartbroken
but still snaps and sends out the image in his viewfinder;
I am gripped by the picture I am trying to grasp
after 20,959 Facebook Shares to get it to me.

I cry out, "Show this boy the Golden Door,
He has what it takes to survive, to strive!"
I tear at our leader's selfish policies,
my muscles contracted and hands clenched in anger.

James R. Ellerston on March 3, 2018
UNHCR Team
Posted March 2, 2018 at 1:40 A.M.
Shared with me on March 3, 2018

The Cost of Knowledge

There was no ticket fee for me to pay for this tonight,
but the four presenters had dearly purchased their place at the table
with a troubled upbringing destroyed by years of war and fear before,
were now exhausted after dredging up years of their painful childhood memories.
for our evening's stunned enlightenment as a community.

A hometown crowd packed auditorium seating, sat on the floor, patiently stood,
as an intense foreign film prepared us to understand maturing adolescents
in wartime Netherlands occupied by dreaded Nazi Germans under Swastikas;
dialogue from four Dutch survivors helped us to understand both---
those who struggled to stay alive and the atrocities committed.

Sundays Pastor risked praying for the Queen; another was shot in his pulpit.
An arrested brother returned from camp as a skeleton, dying ten years later.
We were ordered to remove the loft straw looking for Jews, soldiers, weapons.
Collaborators that were pro-German betrayed our family three times.
Tulip bulbs were eaten like cooked potatoes; and sugar-beets from cows' troughs.

Most babies died in cities during the Hunger Winter; fathers begged us for milk.
The Germans flooded the polder farms; other farmers got the cows.
Fear; "you never saw, never heard, never knew anything"; 18 stayed at our house.
Men set out from the cities for food dressed as women riding tireless bicycles.
The last month the Allies dropped food; first tea bags and cream crackers.

These two men and two women spoke of their families in the Second World War;
the unrelenting hunger, bitter cold, constant anguish, and pain in wartime life;
a chronic lack of food in a small European nation oppressed by foreign soldiers;
after the war leaving the Netherlands and emigrating to the States and Canada;
we heard from some now residing in Pella, "city of refuge", on these shores.

James R. Ellerston
March 5, 2018

The Clock Stopped, Love Went On

our eyes on earth did tear when the tiny one's heart quit beating,
no less loved by the pounding muscle pumps surrounding
in those outside of the internal saline sea in which dwelled the hope
of a new life in the heat of a human body.

egg and sperm conceived in a dish in a medical lab,
taken from the scientific cold to the anatomy of a warm female womb
and growing these few joyous weeks in a wondrous pool inside a mother
until time suddenly ran out, when fluid gushed out.

there was no longer a reason for an anguished wait
for the earthly growth of an infant,
in which a soul of the universe could inhabit
for a few decades detour before returning to reside at home with God.

now grief has graduated so early this cherished being
to hold a position in Heaven teaching of love mixed with pain---
and prayers of grandparents for the miracle baby gone
the remainder of these persons' parental days.

James R. Ellerston
March 9, 2018

Keeping the Faith After the Classroom Bell Rings

he sat on the edge of the single bed in the mental ward
so glad we had driven the miles to see him in the hospital,
face searching for affirmation in our steady eyes--
his body spasming awkward muscle twitches as we talked.

our presence, this traveled distance across the highwayed state
the time spent told him we cared about him so far from home,
a former student of our retired school teaching days--
one for whom we had continued to care all these fly-by years..

we listened two hours to his continuing anguished tale,
his past not always pretty but somehow now more grim;
at departure seeking to improve his future chances our honest goal;
my attorney friend pledged to volunteer to help his struggling soul.

we must continue to look out for people from our decades past,
our love for them does not fade away when formal work days end;
this troubled man's growing children deserve his fatherly goodness;
an effort from caring friends together can save the life of another.

James R. Ellerston
March 12, 2018

Wordless Poetry and Verse Loving Daily

he loves her so deeply,
nightly lying quietly next to her in the darkness;
but the ambition of the manhood inside him
each day tears his scent from her body,
but not her's away from his loving mind
when the chiming ring of the morning alarm awakens him from paradise,
and gets him to move for work,
to leave her lying there alone so early without sunlight.

he packs his lunch in the time-change darkness,
dresses his runner's body in paint-splattered heavy cotton clothes
joins the stream of commuters on three lanes of desperate highway
and returns to a job, a team of workers, money in an account;
he is now a participant in the system, part of the current economy.

he is not so sure of much in his daily life yet,
but continues to go to schooling to learn a skill he hopes to succeed with--
earning income and her respect,
not having people or himself see him as a poor boy again;
he has a means to get a job, pay rent, to survive in years ahead,
with family, her daily approval and continued love.

he does not want to feel the Arizona belly's pangs of hunger,
or the mind's insecurity at the criticism of others again;
he wants to feel the confident athletic security of a thirteen-mile run,
"runners' high" and muscled legs and fast feet in good shoes;
he now has lungs that breathe easily in a heart-filled chest,
weary, soft-spoken at workday's end,
feeling enraptured love before blessed sleep.

James R. Ellerston
March 16, 2018

Arms Are For Hugging

My elder body sits at home in a padded armchair,
but my feet "are" on the asphalt today marching
and I "hold" a sign with hope for a future world
where my grandson can sit safely in a school room.

a world where French shoppers can safely visit a market,
where a *gendarme* will not have to give his life
and swap himself to save someone's family member
and a French nation mourn for him in death.

a world hopes enraged policemen will not put twenty bullets into a man
because he held a cell phone; a frightened someone shouted "gun";
for this young Black breaking glass became a capital death offense,
worthy of a twenty-bullet execution in his grandmother's backyard;
(he bled five minutes on the ground before given any assistance.)

today March 24, 2018 our youth feel empowered to walk and dream;
may their "never again" apply to all our many wrongs;
in France today the French President mourns publicly for one brave man;
in America the President is invisible on the topics of the day that matter.

James R. Ellerston
March 24, 2018

2018 "Superstar" at Near Fifty Years

Because it didn't sound the same as what I had heard,
Easter Sunday night's live broadcast raised flags,
contradicting memories in my mind of college years
and repeated listening to the original recording.

The music was new then, the text controversial,
and the Campus Church "thinkers" amongst us
gathered in the often-flooded concrete hole
of a dank never-to-be-finished bowling alley beneath the Union.

Someone had hauled in their personal portable stereo,
another brought dittoed *Samizdat* librettos to the "rock opera";
afterwards we took the texts back to our dorm room with us,
underground literature brought back by New York students.

As the vinyl LP spun upon the record player,
the music and now 33 rpm proclamation of the life of Jesus
hit the campus and the world challenging imaginative minds
of conservatives who believed the NRSV to be written by God.

On a patient evening sitting on carpet squares on bare concrete
under the glaring nakedness of bare bulbs in a room of echos,
we bared our souls to this new text somehow in the protest era
telling differently the story of the days of the Christ.

Condensed to the limits of four record sides playing into the night,
communing students absorbed the message, in eager silence--
listened to the new melodies, songs, and lyrics set to rock beats,
on an evening not to be forgotten in the long lives of participants.

Purple faded sheets moved with old term papers and yearbooks
were finally cast out in later-live's paring down of basement boxes;
but the brown-sleeved recordings traveled cherished once again
with treasured possessions to the smaller later-life's homes.

James R. Ellerston on the Monday afterwards, April 2, 2018

Central Women's Chorus 2018 Debut

eleven treble voices filling the night
as their words and emotions filled the space;
melodies soared in harmonious voice,
as needs and feelings of young women were articulated.

this chorus sang forth in blended pitch
making the scant audience feel the words;
melodies soared in harmonious voice
as their words and emotions filled the space.

eleven treble voices filling the night,
causing my body to shake with inner feelings
celebrating being alive and human
as coeds stood in a uniform of blue jeans.

making the scant audience feel the words
as needs and emotions of young women were articulated;
truth was given contradicting the worst of mankind's fears;
a gathering told convincingly "You are not alone."

James R. Ellerston
April 4, 2018

Flashing Evening Lights

There was a steady flashing of the lights
red and blue emergency bulbs,
a green street light on an Algona highway;
again tonight while the curly haired son stroked an electric guitar
still playing the concert stage under flashing red, blue, green lights;
in my mind years ago his mother crumpled to the floor murdered,
killed behind the convenience store checkout cash register.

Life for her children was never the same again
after that robber's shot through the evening's quiet--
there and another store in the next city down the highway--
his greed for a few dollars cash his only motive, and fired a gun;
tonight agile fingers flying in adept improvisations in a minor key
in the young man's mental stairway for her to heaven
in gigs for painful years passing by;
she never dead in his heart-- the guitar screams agony on the stage.

In Friday night's awaited performance,
dance balls broke up the red, blue, and green spots into sparkles;
though the lights of the emergency vehicles washed the stage
they did not bring her back to life; she was killed before the lights flashed;
pounding rain drops splashed April windshields outside the venue;
during the time a loaded car waited in a church parking lot;
time over for now when the aged teacher had watched him perform--
checking in on the now-adult once-student on stage making music.

They stood together outside in the windy April rainstorm;
the hail passed over from west to east
while the young man smoked his cigarette,
out on the sidewalk talking to the gray-haired man,
whom he knew had come to watch him play tonight
because he still loved him yet from so long ago;
and his teacher then drove home for over two hours in rain, sleet, and snow
just to share a brief time while his talented guitarist whined pain
under those flashing lights of emergency vehicles washing the stage.

James R. Ellerston   April 13, 2018

A Mobile Army Surgical Hospital at Eddyville-Blakesburg- Freemont
MASH: Much About Soldiers' Honor

There is something paradoxical
about constructing a humorous dramatic play about warfare;
staging that script on stage, documenting with a digital camera–
the contrast shows in dozens of photos,
with adolescent boys both smooth-faced and young men bearded,
girls aged 13 to 19, all working together weeks dramatizing the tragedy
that happens to young men and women
when sent to the front.

Shot-up and maimed by other young soldiers
because of indoctrination in different beliefs,
but miraculously saved from imminent death
by trained nurses and doctors moved about
in mobile medical huts, who with skill and determination
returned a bleeding, battered child to a mother at home,
after the beating blades of whirling choppers
delivered a body in hurried haste to the sterile surgical table.

Decades later we try to find some humor
in our 21st century lives plagued with televised battle--
about the off-duty antics of the miracle workers hanging onto sanity
during their few hours of relaxation portrayed in book, play, TV and film--
in canvas barracks and bars in icy Korea;
limber female dancing bodies
engaging the attention of male doctors with voluptuous nurses,
preserving mental health with the beauty of fantasy and attraction,
the love of humans for another person.

So these growing high school men and women,
develop bodies attractive to each other;
they deal with masculine and feminine issues in their lives,--
on the sports field, voice parts in the choir,
casual clothing styles, gowns and tuxedos at the prom--
determine self identity, and date others in the outreach for another;
this is such a part of life, and joyful or difficult for some teenagers.

To make humor of these subjects--
dating, sexual attraction, deadly warfare, saving bloodied bodies--
requires a maturity and self-acceptance that can be natural
or can be coached into an actor's life;
ideas were portrayed with a satire that was as much painful
as it was humorous on the cafetorium stage;
warfare is a tragedy, may be required, may be a mistake,
can be a waste of beautiful young persons' futures;
learning about the choices for good
that can occur between the firing guns--
illuminated with an audience laugh--
may save a life when a young military person needs inner hope
after being required to kill another in order to survive;
putting on this play whether it is serious or a comedy
brought cast members closer to each other,
closer to their humanity, parents', and grandparents' reality,
helped them understand every veteran they encounter.

James R. Ellerston
after Sunday's play April 15, 2018
April 17, 2018

Diplomacy Set to Music

This week the war may have finally ended
in the peninsula with the joyful dancing across the border line
of the two Korean leaders hand in hand.

On a high school stage filled with talented actors
the body of the martyred mediator was borne under the highway
in a cortege across the concrete jungle battlefield of the gang rumble.

Grief stricken members of the two racial gangs now shared this fault line,
a sudden truce by those who had once celebrated on stage
in youthful dance filled with abandon, spirit, and power their differences.

It was the sense of belonging to two distinct opposing groups
that somehow suddenly came together on the curtained platform
in front of the theater goers with dropped jaws in a filled auditorium.

Viewers breathed through gaping mouth, young men in armies danced,
while on the battlefield, the strong role of Tony, the dreaming mediator,
is smitten with his first beautiful young love across deadly lines of rival groups.

Tragedy, in the centuries old tradition of Shakespearean acting,
became apparent as our Romeo climbed the famous balcony,
loved his Juliet and passed away, a victim of a contemporary gun shot.

Comic relief provided us an awkward scene with the teen boy on her bed,
putting on his sneakers and falling out the tenament bedroom window at dawn,
quietly betraying their consumation of bridal-shop wedding vows.

Throughout, the voice of the maiden Maria floated out tunes
by the genius composer Leonard Bernstein singing for a new boyfriend;
the portrayal of the teen-aged Tony magnificent in slim blue jeans and T-shirt.

The typical American adolescent boy, blinded to reality at love's awakening,
was portrayed with accurate form and angst for his sudden changing desire;
yet innocence still in his clean boyish face singing of young hope and love.

This boyish prince sang forth in a clear resolute voice that made us have faith;
he believed in a better future for himself and his lovely bride;
the audience was led to long ardently for an improved outcome.

Intervention of the store owner "Doc" gave the two lovers hope--
both monetary means to get away from the neighborhood tensions,
and of a new future, through a sermon on life from an elder's perspective.

Feeling love helped Tony soar his voice through melodies and lyrics
until the catastrophic bullet turned the joyful love story
into the daily familiar tragedy of our nightly evening news reports.

The hearts and minds of emotional theater goers once drawn in by song
are again moved by a boy meets girl plot timeless in film and on dramatic stage;
painful concluding scenes still tear at viewers of the repetitive daily chronicles.

James R. Ellerston
April 28, 2018

West Side Story
Indianola High School
April 26, 27, 28, 2018
Maria- Lauren Whtiesitt
Tony- Joey Mathieu
Musical Director- Melody Easter-Clutter
Choreographer- Erin Horst

City Tulip Festival Disrupted

movement in the dark Western clouds;
people celebrate the springtime floral growth
with beds of blooming flowers emphasized;
traditional costumes worn from Netherlands heritage.

wail of loud siren for three minute warning agony;
small young-ones run toward shelter in terror;
parents grasp children by the hand moving to safety;
food stand shutters bang down ending evening culinary pleasures.

amazing miracles of modern radar and weather forecasts
tell us exactly where the midwest tornados are on the ground;
tourists get in cars; locals go to houses with broadcast media maps
and seek out protection in cellars below vulnerable frame houses.

late evening cellphones communicate with family, friends, others
and verify that all appear to be safe in their location;
boxes and colors on the state map move slowly eastward distant
to spoil and threaten someone else around their backyard grill.

James R. Ellerston
May 4, 2018

Only in Pella

blue sky, sunny day, light breezes, thousands of colored tulips;
almost too warm for the heavy Dutch historical costumes and hats;
sworming hive of tour busses and cars from in and out of state--
"where you from" answers "east Texas, Oklahoma, and Missouri".

a sea of teens on the street with friends, mixed with seniors, babies;
couples with hands entwined promenade affection on the sidewalks;
a large crowd brings a diverse zoo of dogs on leashes and in arms;
whole schools of elementary students walk the sunny parade,

cadenced bands in plumed hats march to contemporary tunes;
old carriages, wagons, and harnessed horses evoke the pioneers;
antique autos, tractors, festival royalty travel broom-washed streets;
everywhere curbside blankets, lawn chairs, strollers displaying kids.

in late evening darkness under the glow of light-trimmed buildings
floating thematic clouds glide sparkling past observant applause;
a vibrant downtown event with grandstand stage show and parade--
celebrating moving for religious freedom with an opening prayer.

James R. Ellerston
May 5, 2018

Saturday Spent With Family Friend

sitting high up in free seats on metal bleachers with an agile runner,
I hear a familiar voice announcing festival queens and attendants;
parents and very young black-capped boys wet-wash pavement
re-enacting old Dutch street cleaning for today's throng of tourists.

free grandstand seats are donated by a local industrial factory--
this full-employment town of metal workers and wood workers--
a wealth of history, Christian faith, college academia, and money;
my visitor frequents food stands, pub, beer garden, day and night.

our good times are filled with street conversations with strangers,
meeting veterans, elderly locals in costume, and distant travelers;
"what kind of dog" was requested of the twenty-something couples;
a gala observing motorized floats bedecked with youth in splendor.

a yearly heritage celebration mingling blonde hair and gray beards,
sharing of past and present, future hopes, grandparents' teachings;
I share Tulip Time with a beloved young man, lives wound together;
he easily bends catching scents of vibrant colors in springtime beds.

James R. Ellerston
May 6, 2018

William Penn University Commencement 2018

dignified professors solemnly marched in robes and colorful academic hoods,
followed by joyful young people sprightly moving toward their graduation,
to march across the flag-draped platform proudly to receive honors and diplomas
from a college leader who commands the helm of a dignified Quaker- led university.

founded in 1873 in southern Iowa in an area with Friends churches,
now a long-time institutional heritage extending back more than a century
in the small city of Oskaloosa where my own Quaker ancestors lived in the past;
they washed clothes for the historical figure John Brown and his Kansas-bound men.

our folder for the ceremony describes the opportunity for experiences at William Penn--
liberal arts promoting a Christian viewpoint from a Quaker-focused perspective--
leadership, technology, simplicity, peace-making, integrity, community, equality--
all described beseeching graduates to be true to themselves in living these life values.

we sat across the crowded gymnasium aisle from his sister, mother, and grandmother
during a ceremony in which youth marked the time and influence of becoming an *alumni*;
in our era of life-long learning and extended coursework for multiple degrees,
he has but one *alma mater*, walking across this stage on his path in life, in cap and gown.

James R. Ellerston
May 5, 2018

Slice of Life (Children in Wartime)

customer in the chair, comb and scissors moving;
he had learned to barber in the Netherlands
but later passed a licensure in Iowa years ago;
we gathered and listened to the two men talk in a Pella shop.

questions from a small audience pulled forward the past,
making events of wartime Holland childhood vivid this afternoon;
adults and teenage boys took notes as events years ago unfolded;
a nine year old's memory walked again amongst Nazi occupiers.

as a youth, up early in the morning, leaving home at 6 a.m.;
searching for life-giving daily bread which small boys could steal,
and the good generous German baker by the railroad enabling life;
surplus fresh bread laid on a table near woods sheltering escape.

grab the bread, back into the brush, loaves stuffed in shirts;
questions never asked by mother, glad to feed brothers and sisters
and that her boy was home, unlike the older underground son;
besides school, the constant searching with fear of bullet in the back.

saving of families was a priority of this Dutch barber's father--
one usually thinks of individuals saved-- but 180 families by this man!
in barns, underground tunnels, straw stacks; machine guns fired;
people hauled away, shot if they fell walking, no matter the age.

gnawing hunger, daily, weekly; stealing food from Nazi appropriation;
all of Europe was starving, foodstuffs destroyed, shipped to fronts;
in days of mercy air feeding, a British Lancaster crashed nearby;
a benevolent German General shot, killed, for allowing food drops.

II.

in the leafy backyard of his sheltering home a drama played out;
the ten-year-old boy became an emboldened man,
in an instant entering adulthood;
his father forced at gunpoint to kneel upon the grass;
the boy stared with desperate courage into evil's eyes,
and in cracking pre-adolescent voice resolutely said,
"If you kill him, I will search you down the rest of my days,
and slice your throat from ear to ear!"
this seared into his memory, not any thanksgiving tears,
as the German did an about-face and walked away.

III.

in his mother's sheltering arms the cuddled infant no longer suckled;
the constant lack of food had robbed the woman's nutrition;
the child subsisted on potato water;
motherhood suffered at the soldier's gun held to her child's head;
she had answered "I don't know,"
when from the nearly hysterical mother an answer was demanded
by the ugly, uniformed German,
"Where is your husband, and why is he gone?"
with the gun still at baby's head,
they finally accepted that my mother did not know;
(my father was is the resistance)
and my father and I both lived.

IV.

two young brothers sat next to me on the couch taking notes;
we discussed questions afterwards about how history is taught;
how much detail can troubled American school students tolerate?
in wartime Holland the hungry boy had gone to church,
climbed to the high pulpit and opened the Bible;
he blacked out "thou shall not steal" in the book of Exodus
with tape across the Commandment;
and through wartime theft of food and guns,
lived to tell the tale today.

James R. Ellerston, Henry S. and Henry R.
May 9 and 10, 2018

Visit to Kuyper House: Memory of 1966

Freshmen and Sophomore women competed in presentations
of short operetas with music flowing forth from the piano and voices;
instruments in original songs and dialogue college students wrote;
Pietenpol Cup was a big deal at Central College in the 1960's.

Evening darkness had crept over the neighborhood
as my parents and I searched out the home;
it was a big house where the college friend of my sister lived
on the north side of the Pella street.

Elm trees still graced the campus at that time;
the deadly fungus had not yet choked off the water flowing
up massive dark trunks to leafless branches dancing in the wind,
as we strolled the leaf-strewn sidewalks in late fall.

Brightness flooded our eyes as we climbed the wooden porch
and were welcomed into the family by the front door
as the student classmate of my sister introduced her parents,
and these joyous well-mannered gracious people entered my life.

Light filled the large foyer by the open staircase;
cups of refreshment were offered, then placed in our hands;
father Hospers ran the local music store to supply my music needs;
a gracious pianist by his side, Joyce, lived one hundred years.

James R. Ellerston
May 12, 2018

Christian Riley Garcia R.I.P. May 18, 2018
Sante Fe, Texas High School Hero

I see the vivid image of Christ in a schoolhouse hallway
helping Riley hold closed the door so others might live
when he took a fatal bullet in the line of God's chosen duty.

He did it right for humanity and fellow students,
with God's help holding back the shooter blindly inflicting death,
and at the age of 15, gave up his earthly life for his friends.

This teen became a hero in the eyes of many,
deserving national honor for doing it right on behalf of others--
a John Wayne "American" medal for having "true grit".

This boy wanted to join the military as a man,
now won't see age 18 because he took a stand in harm's way--
stood before a demented gunman's rage with strength from Jesus.

He was with Riley at the door where they continuously stood in love;
He carried his strong spirit to heaven's glories,
when Riley was taken from this strifeful world to dwell with God.

James R. Ellerston
May 22, 2018

My Read in Church Prayer Created Controversy

I am scared;
I want my Mommy;
At the border they took me from my mother--
I was crying--
and they pried me from her arms;
she still has my doll and blanket;
my stomach hurts, I am so lonely.
Where are they taking us?
I hear other children crying.

There is a great silence in the media;
only some good souls on Facebook care about me;
evil men are in charge.

I know there were 5000 of us taken from our mothers at the border;
1475 of us are lost by the government; they don't know where;
Pray for us.

Will Jesus come sit by me in my loneliness ?
When will his wayward lambs be found?

James R. Ellerston
May 27, 2018

Tuned Into the World

At age 13, yards of copper wire were strung around my bedroom,
and hooked to old, heated-up big tubes on a metal chassis;
in its walnut cabinet, this radio delivered music I had never heard;
by turning the knob to "SW" -- shortwave was a window on the world;
and in amongst stations transmitting dots and dashes endlessly
(these high-pitched signals in repetitive code)
was America's unique musical gift to the world.

The Voice of America signal I was able to receive
sent out the sound of the art of Black musicians
in front of recording and broadcast microphones
picking up their unique sound live and on pressed vinyl,
sent out from the station in Virginia-- can't remember where;
but the signal reached this Iowa farm boy even better after dark,
and at the same time reached behind the Iron Curtain,
and to those behind the Wall in Berlin; I knew about that Wall.

This was in my junior high years of science and Charles Dickens;
my weekly allowance spent each week at Don's T.V. and Stereo;
(Don was an alcoholic but his store was a lifeline to me);
one evening my V.O.A. listening was to Black trumpeter Donald Byrd,
backed up by a vocal chorus making "sacred" sounds;
and when my LP came after a few weeks I played it endlessly;
it was on the great jazz Bluenote label, pressed in monaural;
my last album in single-track sound;
at the end of the not-yet-stereo world; only one idea was correct.

Life moved on into high-school years and debate team trips;
there were new friends and playing guitar in groups;
the old tube radio which had sat on spool chests holding my rocks
returned to storage in the attic and when I left home to the dump;
and my shortwave voyage into Cold War politics ended;
President Kennedy was killed in Dallas; no school a day to watch TV;
our nation was embroiled in a domino-theory war across the sea;
my driving the family car became my way to travel the planet.

An elementary school rock collection is now stored in a basement;
spool chests from great-grandfathers general store still by my bed
in my room in another empty-nest house holding a new machine,
giving me a night breath in my present aging life with my spouse;
still a frightening place with music communicating the best there is;
threats of another wall again still divide communities and nations--
America no longer willing to offer amnesty and escape from terror,
a lamp by the golden door and the value of the radio jazz dimmed.

James R. Ellerston
June 6, 2018

First Aid Kit, Saving Souls

Pounding through the ocean spray, our craft came to sudden halt;
our skipper with his hatchet, hacked bodies from the prop;
our turn, ready, we waded waters' drowning depths and windy chop.

I felt the warmth of sacrifice, fingering my neck-strung cross;
when I plunged into the red-stained water,
I hoped my service would be worthy to the Father.

The thickness of courage before me,
I crawled forward on the Normandy land,
in this crucial hour upon cursed sand,

It is my job to quickly move from man to man;
your wounded body I sought to reach
to use the skills they'd tried to teach.

I hoped the red cross on my helmet would protect,
as bullets sailed the noisy air veiled with smoke around;
men dead, maimed, and fatally wounded did abound.

I gave dulling morphine to save you from bodily shock;
we lay in terror behind steel of tank trap's arm,
on fateful mission from weapons' vicious harm.

I lay inside your pool of blood as it soaked my uniform red,
one hand to hold in intestines ripped out this strifeful day,
the other, held my cross, speaking words to the Lord to pray.

A brief few moments and then move on to comfort many youth with faith,
during invasion hell for you and I on this scarred and sacred ground,
beauty of God's sky lost in bloodied beach, crashing crushing sound.

To all people in his verse, the poet forever obligated to preach,
not learned seminary sermons soon forgotten, not heard or needed--
but the lesson of eternal sacrifice for man's future to be heeded.

I still dream of last minutes, blessed with prayers from my own tongue;
yet writing today reminding of history's broad swath in time--
to commemorate with only words, make an effort to use rhyme.

James R. Ellerston
June 6,7,8 2018

Satisfying Garden Salad

one beautiful gentle horse
grazing a little close to the house;
when she had enjoyed the grass,
she got herself back into the barn;
I quietly removed a leather halter,
and brushed her sleek coat.

the peonies in the lawn survived
another day of sunshine;
a vase of blossoms cut and watered
scents up the house;
fragrant permeating smelll
gives the reason for equine avoidance.

James R. Ellerston
from Glenn Henriksen on Facebook
June 13, 2018

In Green Pastures

a peaceful scene today
on the west edge of town;
cows with calves stand
white-faced in the field,
brown coats all matched
as if bought at the same store.

plenty of luxurious grass to eat
munching through the greenness
fenced in by a distant treeline,
a barrier between ground and sky;
(put there by an artist's brush
to set off the white clouds in blue).

there is barbed wire strung across the field,
a truthful end limit to grazing in that direction;
the horned bull has projections above his gentle ears,
models his appetite proudly with a left ear and moist nose
between the wires eating a tall green weed;
swarms of buzzing gnats filling humid June air.

James R. Ellerston
June 17, 2018
photo by Glen Henrikson June 14, 2018

In Remembrance of Me

We remember people
and the people we longest remember
are the people that we remember
helping us on our way--
persons that helped us through a troubled day,
or could be counted-on for a smile, an affirmation,
each time they were seen.

We remember persons who listened to us
and didn't talk through our ideas;
but remembered they were our ideas
and did not try to claim our thoughts as theirs'
because they would not remember the ideas were ours.

I cannot remember people's first names;
give me their last name
and I will file their first name with it;
I will remember their story
and their eyes;
remember this--
when I can't remember you now that you've aged,
it's not because I wasn't interested in remembering you--
but that the filing system got confused.

The cabinet of the mind aging is less plastic now;
never before had it hardened to steel,
to steal away the memories of our past distant time;
these are often remotely stored away;
in now empty vaults that do not remember places,
past times, who persons are-- only feelings.

But your eyes convey remembrance,
remind me of my memory of your soul--
a time long ago, made as recent as yesterday
by your eyes' gleam or sudden flick,
you remembering a certain day;
if there is a memory, a past vision now remembered,
that could be sent with every caring glance--
convey that you remember who I was to you then--
and in that memory love me still.

In this time today in my aging difficulty,
I may not remember you,
or yesterday, this morning, or an hour, even a minute ago;
but when I like your eyes
and the gentle sound of your voice;
your perfume may smell good to me.

James R. Ellerston
June 24, 2018

Legacy

Remember my own daughter married an immigrant,
who came from across the sea;
my grandson sits reading upon my lap,
and with red Ferrari cars for hours will play.

Don't take any immigrant's child away,
a grandpa's heart to break:
and those who collaborate with this inhuman sin,
shall hear the scythes of Hell in eternal din.

There are those who wonder
why this old man should so earnestly care;
but it was every baby's diaper,
I changed, wiped so carefully bare.

Parents and grandparents love tiny infants
they've nourished from cherished wombs;
whose yard that parent was raised in
makes no worldly difference when finally out searching.

Brave loving parental feet will seek wide and far
to find their child a safer home--
no matter a sea, a wide-bedded river
or a tall evil border fence in the journey's way.

James R. Ellerston
June 24, 2018

Thankful Time for Days' End Rest

One packs the car, miles are driven from state to state;
this going home to familiar scenery
as we come closer, does the dog excite;

It is now the sixty-third year I've come from Iowa
to this shore, to this stretch of sand,
a few pine trees, and rustic cabin on this site;

Distance is driven over seat-sore days, and campground nights
with an automobile, trailer, and two pets--
too much for a flight;

We come to this lakeshore village with extended family
and our German Shepherds, "keeping them on a leash",
to keep them from distant people and other dogs which bite;

Our place is in the northern wilderness, Chippewa Forest,
with "by the lake" secured by human thoughtful effort
and decades of muscled fight.

Celebrate the rising sun,
that brilliant gift of gaseous radiance,
summer days warmth, and longer daytime light;

Swim each morning, cook a breakfast,
find warmth and shelter, good food to eat,
bring companions on vacation-- our survival plight;

Raise the mast to voyage away,
secure the billowing sail with lines
and pulleys' wisdom cleated tight;

When all is said and done, an afternoon playing on sand
near water, with my grandson on pristine beach,
is life's greatest delight;

Cloud cast sky racing across earth's dome
blocks the stars in darkening eve,
masks the beauty of heavens' planetary might;

Only electric lamps are gleaming now,
distant shores twinkle across the dancing waves,
brightness stabbing my aging sight;

No moon starts a path around the earth,
in this highway map of velvet blackness,
of day's end falling forest night.

James R. Ellerston
June 29, 2018

After the 4th
(Keep Them Safe On The Highway)

There were grandkids on the widow's beach next door,
playing in the water in bright sun upon the gradual shore;
wave swept sand is quiet now, no noisy kids in sight;
young family's blue pickup left for Ohio, unheard, gone in the night.

Nine hundred miles driven, in the dark, all day, back sore and more;
home for a lakeside holiday, for neighbors' and grandma's delight;
so very worth miles of lane-changing hazard,
fast food, busy Interstate highways' fight.

We travel here, so many of us, from distances states away;
miles airlines flown, or on far roads with cherished beloved dogs;
from Virginia, Florida, Indiana, New Jersey, Colorado, Oregon, more
winter homes were left behind, for summer's shoreside stay.

To own a forest cabin dream
throughout life that is somehow always ours;
each season with family in the pines--
spending life's most blessed hours.

James R. Ellerston
July 7, 2018

Tell Them Your True Feelings
(So Glad You Are My Friend)

In the morning's brightest sunrise,
    when alive this one day more;
Clouded mist swirling on blue lake,
    or life's choppy distant shore;
Green pines, or snowy peaks,
    I rise to another daily fight;
But with my phone in palm I feel secure,
    connected in time's love.

There could be a miracle,
    in a message sent with moving thumb;
Black printed brief short sentences.
    sent thru satellites' orbiting hum;
Warm spoken voices from far away days,
    over handy cell phone calls;
When between willing distant persons,
    with tall towers above one conveys love.

We are not further apart,
    than that small microwave box;
Warm electronics with which
    we can send isolated thoughts;
Can reach out to distant friends with no effort,
    their present emptiness to dissolve;
Search out, find obituaries of a heavenly family,
    not dead, still with our earthly love.

There could be a miracle,
        in a message sent with moving thumb;
Black printed brief short sentences.
        sent thru satellites' orbiting hum;
Warm spoken voices from far away days,
        over handy cell phone calls;
When between willing distant persons,
        with tall towers above one conveys love.

There is an urgent responsibility in the night,
        when your phone wakes you with a ring;
To respond with kindness then renewal,
        when the message could hope bring;
Call them from decades ago--
        parent, student, roommate, or friend;
Punch in a number, dial a distant shore,
        save someone with pain inside with love.

There could be a miracle,
        in a message sent with moving thumb;
Black printed brief short sentences.
        sent thru satellites' orbiting hum;
Warm spoken voices from far away days,
        over handy cell phone calls;
When between willing distant persons,
        with tall towers above one conveys love.

James R. Ellerston
July 7, 2018

Summer Night

windows are open to night's moving air
and a sound of waves breaking on the beach;
he lies bare-chested upon his simple bed,
feeling breeze caress his tanned skin and sun-washed hair,
hands moving on desires' flesh, mind free from care.

positioned lying now on body's side against a pillow long,
a cotton body soft sack provides comfort and emotional support;
hold that position of less pressure, ache, and stress;
now dream a while more for tired mind's sake,
no stolen thoughts from wakeful hours restlessness to make.

old and young alike need long hours of sleep,
soothed by traveling wind across familiar bedtime waters deep;
toilet needs and desires' throbs so frequently might awake;
before mornings' arising shining sun
his days ambitions can he make.

a boy loves his manly muscled body and rested easy feelings
as night's quiet dark hours fade away
and renewing hopes the returning lights of daytime bring;
his wholesome flesh might become aching "morning wood",
and thoughts of desire that in minds of young men spring.

James R. Ellerston
July 8, 2018

Facebook Pastoral Photo

In the distance above the fence line trees,
the yellow "M" sails above green smokey slopes;
a sign of "golden arches" flouts its announcement
above blue mountain haze.

In the area near a graveled road and barbed wire fence,
brown and white, and black and white, cattle graze;
across the grass two animals lie resting on the grass,
splendid in the sun.

Civilization is given away by lights reaching upward on poles,
and the McDonalds' building visible through the forest
stalks its prey by suggesting sympathetic hunger
to my rumbling stomach.

James R. Ellerston
July 18, 2018

Thailand Cave Rescuer Dies

They raced to drain the water
to save a young soccer team;
twelve youth trapped below in a cave,
mud, water, doing well, spirits still running high;
rescuers found the boys and coach on dry ground--
and brought them food and hope..

In an overnight mission the Thai Navy Seal died,
working to replace oxygen canisters
in the Tham Luang Nang Non waterlogged cave;
(where the boys are two and one half miles in
from the cave entrance through winding tunnels);
rescue workers started teaching the Thailand team to swim and dive.

A round trip from command post to those trapped now taking six hours;
ideally water levels could be lowered to the boys' waists--
so the age eleven to sixteen year olds could walk out;
scuba gear would make an extremely dangerous trip
through the dark and dangerous waters;
(not all on the soccer team could swim).

A search was on to find faster ways to pump out the water,
while the boys were taught wearing a scuba mask
and to get comfortable breathing;
there was an international effort in the rescue;
the former Thai Navy Seal died of a lack of oxygen--
the breath of his dreams slowly smothered, his life freely given for others.

A rescuer had died, but there was no change in the dynamic;
a monsoon season was on its way; the mission did finally succeed.

James R. Ellerston
Summer 2015

Rescuing the Thailand Soccer Team

after ten nights in the labyrinth cave
the retired Navy Seal had come down;
he told the twelve boys and their leader
that they had been found;
that help was on the way,
and if they would wait, they'd get out another day;
at the cave mouth parents, public, and media cheered,
gave this discovery an overwhelming "hurray";
technical skill and courage through water and mud,
through night-black darkness eventually found the way;
their bodies were weakened from the long ordeal,
said the medic after arrival with supplies, safe food for a meal;
with only a dozen hours to the next big rain,
to remove the boys safely was a timely race;
the downpour had stopped, a lull in the storm,
gave rescuers a chance to keep them all safe;
young boys had left bicycles at the jungle cave entrance
before monsoon rains trapped them in the nooks and crannies;
hope given by an international team of rescuers--
from world-wide they came, brought faith and to parents gave,
over days, that with skill and courage their sons they would save.

James R. Ellerston
Summer 2018

II.

Because of Sgt. Major Saman Kunan, retired, from the Thai army,
twelve young lives were saved from a cave's subterranean spaces;
he selflessly gave his life to bring them from the waters' flood;
he died without oxygen, gift of breath, crawling amidst rock, mud.

These twelve Thailand boys from cave's flooded passages freed,
all alive to feel bright mornings' gaseous sun infernal rise--
see silver moon's voyages across nighttime star filled skies--
after days of continuous darkness below in unbroken endless days.

Divers from many nations went the distance, over and over again,
swam miles with boys so incredibly brave, leading them to safety,
skillfully taught them to swim and breath from a tank--
before parents could give up, before hopes for rescue sank.

They led them through miles of perilous journey
from the hazards of the flooded cave;
people of several tongues communicated and understood together;
with one united goal-- the boys to coach and save.

Individual ambulances rolled reaching good medicine and care,
then a world's celebration of youthful pluck and bravery,
divers' skills had rescued all, inspired in their task--
get them out alive, teach all to be courageous, to swim and dive.

James R. Ellerston
July 10, 2018

Western Pond

Held in by gray split-rail fences snaking through grasses,
beneath the pine-swept rise of hills,
riderless horses cross the long growth on the valley floor,
not seeing the sky-reflecting water as an obstacle.

They plunge into the cool liquid with splashing hooves;
heads kept high enjoying the coolness of the stream held back,
before the log-jammed wooden dam holding water deep
for months of summer heat and yellowed seeding plants.

There will be late season's growth here yet,
before the Aspens put on their golden autumn coats.

James R. Ellerston
July 11, 2018

At Mayo Clinic in Rochester: Hope

on the marble floor outside the banks of elevators, he sat,
directed in the wheelchair,
silent in his athletic shorts and tennis shoes,
pushed along by his mother between the marble walls.

he displayed a stubborn but determined expression
on a boyish face with a slight mustache,
tossed long brown hairs on his scalp,
dark straight hairs on calves and shins.

today dressed in a gray hoodie pulled up over his head,
he's trying to hang on to his adolescent life;
looking at him one couldn't identify his illness;
this, my first really emotional view of a sick teen at Mayo.

parent and son wait outside the row of elevators for a car,
while we went to the ninth floor for a simple x-ray;
one instantly knows why they came here for treatment;
the young man and his mother are seeking "Hope".

James R. Ellerston
July 18, 2018

Equine Parable

Two horses converged in a yellowed grass field--
they shared their food between them;
they displayed care and affection for each other
when the pasture ground did not provide enough
for the tethered horses staked-out with halter and rope.

In their one spot allotted on this earth
hay provided by the caring rancher is available to both;
yet one free-running horse transported food to the other,
displaying its speedy gait and prance in traveling the delivery;
they shared the nutritious sustenance.

A generous provider graciously gave to the needy other;
one animal obtained and hurried the food to the hungry equine,
running across the dry pasture sharing alone with zeal,
bearing more than it could need and devour itself;
they broke hay together-- one giving with honest generous love.

With nesting birds, the mother birds feeds the hatchlings;
humans should learn more from the kingdom of animals;
two horses converged in a yellowed grass field--
they shared their food between them, they broke hay together,
and the beauty of the stars was displayed on their faces.

James R. Ellerston
July 25, 2018

Faulty Facilities

the family goes out to a restaurant to eat;
this is a rarity to be at the same place,
at the same time,
and have a sit-down meal together.

my youngest leaves the table;
he needs the restroom;
he leaves his cell phone behind;
a lot of time passes without his return.

someone from our party goes to check on him;
more seconds grow into absent minutes;
soon two return;
they are in a fit of laughter.

it seems that my son was locked in the restroom;
after he used the plumbing for relief,
the door had stuck shut
and wouldn't budge.

he had pulled off the knob,
and for him there was no release
until someone came to help;
they returned to the table afterward chuckeling.

at sixty-eight I propped the door open,
and did not shut it fully
while meeting my own urinary needs;
needed more often by me than my boy who is thirty.

James R. Ellerston   August 8, 2018

Crayons Melting In The West Side Window

I.

grandson comes to the family lake place in Minnesota,
came by plane from Salt Lake City,
small jet from the Twin Cities to Brainerd;
he rode in a car to get here;
played on the beach each and every day--
buckets of beach toys--
shovels, rakes, sand forms, a sieve;
yellow, blue, and green
with water pouring from the small containers,
splashing on toes, hair, face, and the blue shirt;
wind blew cold on the wet fabrics
until the three-year-old's small body
was cooled down;

in a hooded towel, brown with the head of a monkey,
all wrapped around the shivering body
still playing by the waves;
and the water rolled-in underneath the dock;
two pails on the wood now piled with the toys;
time to go to the cabin,
leaving a wake of clutter behind.

II.

he went away with his Mama,
left yesterday to fly home to Utah,
to his Italian grandparents from Rome;
a cell phone message said they had arrived,
home safely again to Salt Lake City.

III.

my grandson left his presence behind,
strewn about the cabin;
DUPLO blocks in "trucks and train",
a big yellow art book of Van Gogh paintings;
there was a Charlie Brown and Snoopy DVD;
a record player in wind-up glory
left a depression in the seat
of the level sofa where he sat next to another Grandma;
the barn-shaped book holder from his mama's Bible school,
pressed into service as a garage for plastic cars
graces the coffee table in the upstairs playroom;
next to the small electric piano
(now turned off and unplugged for winter);
triangle shaped crayons are in a window sill
and at work on big sheets of paper
strewn about the dining room;
bright colors in circular patterns
adorn large sheets of artwork left behind;
a single forgotten Matchbox car
is found behind a chair
before the vacuum cleaner's swath,
and purge of dog hair and pattern blocks;
there are things left behind--
a package of unopened water colors,
a group of new brushes, unused;
sheets of paper that escaped the vigorous coloring;
a last parcel of Playdough delivered by UPS
disappeared in the cabin hustle,
the moving of materials to accommodate family members.

IV.

there is an ache in the hearts
of two grandparents' lives,
soothed by the paths of clutter left behind
from chains of interaction between family--
parent, grandparent, aunt, uncle, nephew, friends--
people important over decades in summer lakeside living,
a sixty-third summer for a grandparent
growing older and weaker, trying to keep it all together;
enjoy another season of neighborhood fish fries,
more tubing, swimming, sailing, and music making.

V.

one misses the young toddler on the beach,
adolescents in the water;
the young man sitting in dock chairs with his girl,
trying to muster courage for the future;
the two cousins pick up the ten-cent snails
and earn money for the trip to Duluth with grandparents;
they dive constantly into the water hunting,
to earn money from their uncle;
neighbor children have a net and goggles are borrowed;
beach toys of a toddler seem small in teen boys' hands,
but they are more careful about putting them on the dock;
plastic makes toys for all ages at the lake;
snail harvesters with goggles feel like the industrial revolution,
now arrived with increases in productivity and income,
and ease of labor to amass product;
sun glistens on the water, a head pops up from the surface;
a youth dives for shells, resurfaces and the pail fills;
at day's end they take turns counting the snails;
sun shines, the elder sits out of the sun,
while the adolescents try to tan and lay out on the dock;
the uncle will need to make a trip to the bank to get cash;
they will search for gaming cards to entertain themselves
with phantasy games popular with today's youth;
there is a truth demonstrated here--
if teens are payed they will make good workers;

James R. Ellerston
August 8, Revised November 8, 2018

Examination Trauma

Alarms go off at sunrise;
three cars leave the cabin by the lake;
my son went north to the Clinic Same Day Surgery
for an invasive medical procedure-- the colonoscopy;
I am in a third vehicle as the two apprehensive parents drive
a familiar road once again, to be there in the waiting room;
the sign outside the building was daunting,
"Radiation, Oncology, Same Day Surgery";
a pleasant girl walks us through the maze to the waiting room;
I balance my coffee cup and write my journal.
my son's patient number moves on a color-coded electronic chart;
on the wall it lists the doctor's names,
and stages of the events behind closed doors.

The sterile waiting room is quiet;
adults stare at cell phones, read paperback novels;
those sipping stainless coffee cups read E-books on tablets;
a flat screen TV drones golf courses, commercials, news flashes;
sunshine projects vertical blind patterns on white walls;
walls graced with outdoors pictures in frames, blue mats always;
there are camera shots of loons on air-brushed forest lakes.

One sits and waits;
time is long in passing;
authoritarian newscasters drone on;
the gal works behind the sliding window at her counter;
black hands crawl the rotation of an analog clock on the wall,
behind rows of equipment on a busy desk;
my son's number advances on the electronic display;
we wait.

We call the neighbors to have them walk the dog;
one never gets him, only his answering machine--
but he called back;
all will be watched over by good friends.

It will be my boy who goes under the gas,
while the doctor moves his camera eye,
and sees in the dark caves of the bowels;
hopefully no signs of things that should not be seen--
signs of disease that might scare our inner soul,
and parental hopes for life's extended pleasure days.

James R. Ellerston
August 9, 2018

Berlin Airlift: A Model for Today

I tried to explain to the impatient teenage boy
about planes landing every minute--
and 40,000 people showing up on the weekend
to build an airfield they needed not to starve that winter--
women working wearing high heels,
because they were the only shoes they had saved from the bombing.

One pilot had only two sticks of gum
and broke them for waiting children, in half that first day,
and not one kid in the group held out a expectant hand for one,
one of only four pieces;
but they saved torn pieces of gum wrapper in china closets,
near the china for the next twenty-five years
so they could smell the flavor, over and over again,
remembering someone had cared in their time of need for freedom.

I don't know if teens ever read the story of the Candy Bomber;
there was an autograph copy of the book from a flea market I gave one;
I tried-- he said he wanted to understand me--
but I said I was very complicated;
he left the book behind when he went home.

It is a great human tale of beautiful people doing their job right;
those heavily loaded planes flew on through the dark of night
with bags of coal for winter through fog
and through rain and snow in the early morning hours--
and so that the milk in glass bottles would be on the table
for the children of the city; it was about children's hearts then,
winning minds to our side in West Berlin during the Cold War.

If the planes flew off course, the Soviets fired on them;
but they had to fly on in any weather to prevent starvation;
one of the great victories of the human heart, and what can be done,
the airlift puts Puerto Rican hurricane relief to shame;
we had the will to do then, but not now.

James R. Ellerston   August 9, revised November 10, 2018

The Cell Phone Might Ring

Yesterday, the cell phone reports
from my daughter
a strong heartbeat,
and adequate growth for the age
of the little one within her womb;
my eyes blink tears of happiness.

I feel her apprehension of the chance of loss,
an anticipation that the knells of death
could claim this young one also;
we as a family could be denied the joys
of diaper changes, holding bottles, and stroller rides--
rides down the endless sidewalks of life,
on always sunny afternoons.

I need no clouds on my horizons;
I need little feet running on the beach's sand,
splashing at the shore's edge,
all my future remaining years.

James R. Ellerston
August 9, 2018

My Grandson At Play

a small orange traffic cone
guards the race track for toy cars;
an ambulance scoots the floor,
its doors opening and shutting;
an orange school bus drives its route,
making frequent stops on the dining table;
(its route belongs on carpets);
the dog hates the sound of the "engine".
the little forward gear charged with energy
by backing the vehicle and then "letting go"
as the vehicle sprints across the road head.

left behind here, there is "Silly Putty" from Olivia,
to stretch between two laughing pairs of hands,
pulled to the maximum
of young lungs' giggling till breaths' exhaustion--
the colors mixed together,
they make a blended gray;
but the colors can't be separated out again;
neither can the laughter of the two--
despite the twenty years of age spread--
in this, a morning of good play.

James R. Ellerston
August 9, 2018

Today's Unsettled (Weather) Conditions

easy haze on distant shoreline treeline;
is it raining over there, across this pond?
gentle undulations splash the sandy beach;
all is gray, sky, rain, lake reflection.

one sits with coffee cup and pen;
restless German shepherds pace their kennels
and emit long winsome howls;
they rarely bark, but sing together.

I await the rain; this morning it never happened;
fishermen trolled the lake in misty morning patient hopes;
neighbors' visiters impatiently walking the dock--
look quizically at the weather question.

after lunch the next-door guests venture into swimming;
an older boy in the water and breeze floats on a tubing toy;
cloudy skys and flapping flags drive them inside;
all is gray, sky, smoke, rain-not-yet, wave sounds on the shore.

my customary late afternoon bath was before dinner;
the neighbor boy, age ten, asked thirty questions;
I did my usual underwater dive and shampoo--
usual cream-rinse followed by repeated submersions;

again an orange sun in a smokey western evening sky;
a faint orange streak across the rippling surface waves;
a light breeze, few mosquitos, even fewer flies;
an observant chair on the deck as overcrowded boats cruise.

daily a small propeller plane beats away the quiet dusk;
tattered national and MIA flags wave from neighbors' poles;
an improperly flown modern Deutsch flag flies beneath America;
still today history and politics mar even northern natural beauty.

James R. Ellerston
August 19, 2018

Artistic Life-Saving Masks

masks have had differing purposes throughout history;
to heighten dramatic artistry in plays,
and have ghoulish designs on halloween revelers,
Carnival and Mardi Gras dancers in the streets.

masks may have a more serious purpose--
to hide disfigurement from natural causes,
or as in Dumas story, to imprison in an iron restriction;
or to enable men to socially function after wounds of war.

it takes an incredible artist to create the disguise
to help an injured man return to life after warfare--
to mold thin copper to bone and face, and paint
this to match soldiers' skin tones, and did it two hundred times.

Anne Coleman Ladd did this so the woman they loved
could still find pleasure in the company of their returning soldier;
in the era of WWI before reconstructive plastic surgery,
the wounded warrior had little option.

the human race emphasizes beauty and normalcy,
race and color issues aside, people need familiarity,
people need recognizable facial images and seek them out,
after events of misfortune and warfare, need to return home again.

Anne Coleman Ladd was an American Artist with a mission,
and she painted on copper for the ordinary soldier;
today big-brother has facial recognition software for cameras;
and she may have pioneered today in 3D printing of prosthetics.

she made 185 masks for soldiers
before returning to her American home,
returning to her life as an artist
and being awarded by the French in 1932.

she went to Paris in 1917, an American artist;
with the help of the Red Cross she made the masks,
Chevalier of the French Legion of Honor
recognized he contributions to the lives of her fellow men.

one's relationships with others is so dependent
on the relationship of personality with facial expression;
she restored an illusion of imagined normalcy for the veteran--
now with willingness to present himself at home.

that news to mother, wife, family that he was alive--
reliving the normalcy of life after cannon, shrapnel, and flame;
she worked at recreating the handsomeness of a young man,
attempting at sculpting the beauty that God had created.

James R. Ellerston
August 21, 2018

On Minnesota Avenue In My Mind

a cloudy day at the lake, but no rain;
a hazy day on the Main Street of town;
a fruitless browse of an Antique Mall;
it is a fuzzy day for my mind;
thoughts come slowly with hesitation--
through a blur that wants to sleep,
making congestion and pain fade away.

James R. Ellerston
August 23, 2018

The Day Wakes Up

the day wakes up with morning light,
a soft ripple of sound upon the roof
of light rain falling to awaken the day;
drops on the steel arrive with gentleness.
reinvigorate vegetation, the surrounding trees and grass
outside the lakeside cabin--
where people gather around the breakfast table
and sip their cups of "too hot",
the strong, dark roast coffee.

James R. Ellerston
August 24, 2018

Searching for the Tools of Words

not a good day, my mind hurts;
actually in the Walmart there was actual pain--
the shelves were just too stimulating;
but I had to find my bold #10 poetry writing pens;
among the shelves of office and school supplies--
finally finding them in packages of two and four
amongst the Crayola products,
the colors of watercolor markers.

Stubborn me must have my select #10 Bold pen--
for the flow of ink across the page;
it feels good with an old man's arthritic hand;
with my broken thumb still sore--
it hurts to use a cheap "stick" ballpoint;
I like the rubber hand grip,
these are still the pen for me.

some days it is difficult for me to shop the merchandise-filled,
cluttered aisles, and shelves of the Walmart store;
this day my wife drove me in the car,
as I dozed away the road home,
conversing, thinking,
waiting to put pen on paper.

James R. Ellerston
August 25, 2018

John McCain the Fighter Embarked Yesterday

Death is such a lonely thing,
something not necessary to experience alone,
whether on the cruel battlefield at bullets' whim,
or in a hospital bed at medicine's miracles failed;
we might be surrounded by family, friends, or fighting buddies--
on fields of conflict red poppies may grow in shell-churned earth,
blooms stand tall on rooms' window sills showing someone loves.

Life's brief years are contained in a fluid-filled body and mind--
flesh which can be imprisoned for a time,
held in captive place and hit upon
by the mean rashness of muscle-driven stick
or a mind hit upon by evil use of words and voice, deprived sleep,
to wear down the body beautiful ,
or idealistic thoughts of the human mind and soul.

Eventually tired, worn down by poor nutrition, prolonged solitude--
eventually even the courageous in time may later stop treatment,
may say "enough" and stop the march of painful medicine,
may decide within their brain's cellular matter--
to enter the silence and peace and experiencing death,
voyage away, joining the cosmos and stars of the heavens,
slipping away from their anchorage on this life-sea earth.

James R. Ellerston
August 26, 2018

Neil Simon Passed

his bright mind lit up the stage
with playwright's dramas;
the struggles and dialogues
of middle class characters
in daily settings and dreams;
dialogue and humor of actors
portraying people who could be us,
who were like you and me;
they acted on stages brilliantly illuminated
by lines of his characters;
when his life curtain was drawn,
his ninety-one year run ended on earth;
his brilliant pen laid down,
the lights of the theatre world dimmed again.

James R. Ellerston
August 26, 2018

From the Land

Like veterans of any war
who survived the battles in body,
but not the war in mind and spirit,
he never talked about it to his children--
never said a word about his parents' farm loss in '36.

The only grandson of Scottish immigrants,
he eventually became the heir--
a grandnephew, not in direct family line;
a hefty purse of federal tax redeemed,
what his aunt had hoarded and saved, which came to him.

As a young boy he went to country school,
won spelling bees and declamation contests,
played on a fretted violin and a basketball team;
he was surrounded by gardened flowers at his home
and in the yard of his grandmother.

Graduating high school early,
at sixteen he attended the local junior college--
maybe he lived away from home, in the county seat;
his only comment about his father was,
"He was a better carpenter than farmer".

To this day an internal debate wages between my sister and me;
She tells that our grandmother's family was cheap--
and wouldn't put up money for crucial payments on the mortgage;
my mother told that the money given was spent on cattle feed;
the cattle market fell and the farm was gone; Depression scored.

In the blizzard winter of '36 they moved out;
there are pictures of my grandparents in a small rough home--
that later became our milking barn, then garage;
the crafted house that Grandpa built was moved off the land, too;
my father drove by it repeatedly on State 9; he never said a word.

From that day on my father farmed the fields of his mother's family;
he ploughed the soil and shoveled grain; supported them;
an evergreen grove his parents planted still in view across the fence--
reminded him of better times, a life that might have been;
to his parents' care he was devoted, working long hard days.

Farmer exempted, sole support of parents, he later built them a house;
he missed fighting in the Second War;
a good conversationalist he sold many War Bonds, a metal tag tells,
to enable neighboring sons to fight across the seas;
later met and married my pianist mother, a teacher at the school.

He never trusted a mortgage again, not for land or farm;
but did buy a Minnesota lake cabin for cash he had saved;
made sure his children knew how to swim and dance,
school and college a goal set in sight, not to "have to farm";
they studied music like their great aunts and mother.

Throughout my own growing years an unused windmill groaned--
electricity was now on the farm, later heated the house;
water was pumped, giant motors dried the grain in bins;
now farmstead buildings and house are torn down, buried;
during spring, in the hilltop grove, purple phlox still blooms.

James R. Ellerston
September 3, 2018

Thomat Visit 2018

gray skies dominated the time spent here,
day after passing day with only splashes of sunshine at most;
light rains falling in sleepy afternoons' naps on old beds,
snoring periods occupying the after-lunch drowsy minutes,
re-energizing from morning reading and writing.

tall dark-barked trunks dominate the yard with forest shadows;
green boughs obscure the lake of placid water deep;
no breeze, no waves lap here; there is no stoney beach--
water meets a shoreline of encroaching greenness;
green lilies blooms dominate the shallows of this spring-fed pond.

our aging bodies have not ventured down the incline
steeply leading to the cedar dock on iron poles;
reaching out friendly into depths like an expectant "shaking hand";
if there were sunshine my white-skinned body might lay there,
upon the boards seeking nature's heat into aching limbs.

there is no lawn mowed here, between the downed logs
left by the power company, saws blazing their wilderness path;
there was a desecration of the natural woods beneath their wires,
this swath of poles bringing the modern conveniences of electricity.
to our place of beauty hidden up a long gravel drive.

quietness pervades this green-leafed primeval mansion,
set aside as inherited for two family's pleasure and recreation;
a "money pit" always with a fix-it list for carpenters and plumbers;
things like roofing, hot water, flush toilets, propane heat, lighting
stand between us and a camping experience, now all but primitive.

James R. Ellerston September 4, 2018

Stormy Weather

thunder rolls cadences throughout the woods;
parades of lightning flash against curtaining sky;
music of soft rhythmic rain beats on forest leaves;
wind accented drops drum on steel roofing
driving the dog to sleep safely at my wife's shoeless feet;
life's passing daily patterns concluded with a dark evening finale.

James R. Ellerston
September 4, 2018

At the Neighborhood Corral

We drive by so often on the way to town for groceries;
for years there have been ponies in the pen;
one always gazes and searches out of curiosity,
sometimes seeing only an empty standing yard.

It is muddy today from the late afternoon rain;
our vision today was of a young colt prancing joyfully;
an entire paddock stands empty for his impromptu dance;
finally sunshine frees him from the confines of his stall.

Yesterday the man who lives there was astride a horse,
a small white horse with bridle and saddle;
in the center of the red clay field he commanded gently,
using bridle straps on the back side of the neck.

The rider guided the horse into very tight circles
and gave a sharp glance toward our slowly rolling car;
he gave a neighborly wave with his free hand,
the other reining the animal, training it for riding.

James R. Ellerston
September 6, 2018

How My Day Passes

There is this dog on the couch in the cabin,
and he sleeps in my bed throughout the night--
a body pressed against my welcoming back,
seeking out security and warmth.

He has a ball that he plays with here,
sometime stores between the cushions near--
barks and scratches when he wants it tossed,
it rolls across the room thrown by a master bossed.

One can tell by the sound when he chews the toy,
fetches it from carpet or dog dish where it fell--
one spends a lot of vacation with a stick for underneath-retrieval
of a ball thrown again, bouncing across, causing an upheaval.

He puts the item eagerly down, stands looking, eyes waiting,
to encourage his family to throw it again, baiting;
with a swift kick of the foot it's rolling toward the door;
if person tired, or pet wants to eat, no desire to chase any more.

James R. Ellerston
September 7, 2018

One Wonders

When we drive by decaying buildings
in a field someone once called home
we think about the energy that built them
and the people who lived there,
moved on long ago.

Wood now turned gray in endless days of sun and rain;
metal roofs orange-rusted that survived the storms;
no groves of hungry-stove firewood from growing trees abounds;
a desolate loneliness, emptiness,
quiet all surrounds.

Far wide horizon and blue sky inspired dreams
and persons' work ethic to rise at light of dawn--
to take this isolated spot on the challenging prairie
and raise one's kids,
laboring to make a family farm.

James R. Ellerston
September 9, 2018

Scottish Ancestors: Alexander Welsh

my grandmother's father came from Scotland
    far across the sea,
farmed his prize sheep in Iowa
    near the Hoprig and Jack Creek throng;
built a house upon a hill
    and big red barn so strong;
raised his wool amidst Iowa corn fathering child after child,
    not then seen as wrong;
sent his sheep to the Chicago Fair in '33
    for all the world to see;
with the animals my father rode the railroad boxcar,
    as happy as could be.

James R. Ellerston
September 9, 2018

Ancestors: Perkins Stores

Great-grandpa Perkins ran a cluttered mercantile
    and lived above the sales' floor;
sold bolts of cloth, cheese, and crackers,
    fresh Saturday-night popcorn outside the store;
things came in wood boxes, metal cans, tea in tin-lined chests;
    in my youth the saved containers were our play-things;
Grandma Carrie and her sisters went to college at Buena Vista,
    and met their husbands before the War;
graduated with earned Bachelor degrees, unusual in that day,
    before their husbands went off to Europe's fray.

James R. Ellerston
September 9, 2018

Ancestors: in Rockwell City, Iowa

sixteen days after great-great-grandpa Mattison came home,
    he'd survived the Civil War to die in pneumonia's bed;
his son Byron Mattison came to Mr. Rockwell's City by the tracks,
    on the prairie of tall grass and marsh;
he founded a newspaper named for the county
    as a strong Republican and civic advocate;
later flipped a coin deciding to collapse his daughter's lung,
    when tuberculosis ravaged Mary's music teaching undone;
my mother's father returned from the horrors of far-off France,
    his sisters ran the presses while he served in the Great War;
alto-vocalist Mildred kept the family home
    raised big gardens many years to feed the family throng;
cared for her invalid mother in the family home,
    giving up her university training in song;
provider Lillian taught Latin and ran the high school library,
    many years of grammar and geography, books on shelves;
these good people raised my mother in their home
    when the long Depression came along;
we ate there many a Sunday meal in my own growing years,
    reliving good times, play clothes mended, books read in love.

James R. Ellerston
September 9, 2018

Ancestors: Canadian Prairies and Matteson Family

My mother-in-law's father shone in school,
    auburn hair near purple;
He studied music at Lawrence College in Wisconsin,
    in Appleton, on the Fox River's stormy banks;
Guy, first in his family to graduate from college,
    was met at the ceremony by his brother Will;
afterward drove-off together to Canada "giving away free land",
    homesteaded with Saskatchewan soil to till;
married his life-long spouse from choir at Davidson Church,
    three children blessed this union;
grain dust eventually drove him back to Illinois,
    an honest salesman to become.

James R. Ellerston
September 9, 2018

Soft Raindrops, Brittle Tears

soft raindrops splash the lake,
but one must wade in anyway;
a detour on the patio rescues wet blue jeans,
takes them inside to avoid the showers;
a brisk northern breeze starts cooling down the air.

a bed has been moved downstairs for a beloved friend;
stair climbing is not within her range of motion--
will the lake satisfy her bathing needs?
probably not, some are not easily convinced
cold lake water is cleaner than the rusty well.

man makes machines to reduce the hardness of household water;
but nothing lessons the grittiness of the barbs we hurl
toward each other getting through daily life,
some days are clouded, our thoughts are easily angered;
no leaking faucet drips softly enough to soothe our mind.

blue gas flames burn in a corner tile-backed stove
amongst ceramic logs, to make a thing of beauty;
an emotion of love may flare in our hearts in an easy-chair-life--
but it is the windy days when cold drafts of efforts prevail,
that make us desire another's warmth to blanket our days.

James R. Ellerston
September 19, 2018

Sculpture in a Florida school and around the country
does not invoke a rushed student-trod hallway;
yet a mere photograph of the small bronzed boy
brings picture viewers to sobbing shaking agony--
What must it be to confront this devastating vision daily?

No "David", but equal in story-telling,
this contemporary simple statue of a sheltering child
could be any Midwest tornado drill, an actual storm,
might be a school-shooter drill,
or exist in the Cold War mind of an aging grandparent.

For this poet of nearly seventy years
futile memories from the Cold War are evoked;
in weekly drills school students practiced atomic salvation--
the futility of hiding under their school desks
seeking shelter from the blast of the A-Bomb.

Block basement rooms stocked with food and water;
directions from Civil Defense in pamphlets;
gold and black signs on the outside of numerous buildings,
emergency broadcast over television--
all destroyed the secure childhood of my own youth.

If these students had responsible parents
a provisioned fallout shelter would have been built,
where one could outlast the decay of radioactive fallout
to emerge into the nuclear winter "Twilight Zone" world that was left;
a new type of society where you had to be willing to kill neighbors.

It would have been necessary to keep contamination out
to protect one's children from the invisible silent killer;
a parent would have fired the gun at his door--
saving his family while hoarding food for his own;
this poet learned to operate a Geiger Counter at school.

Timelessness in art is so rare
but this simple evocation of tragic lost childhood security
depicts several decades of internal pain in this poet's mind;
anguish and agony in last evening's special broadcast--
was yet but another raucous clamor in politics.

Unfortunately this great art was subjected to recent politics--
and while parents' pain was real in every child's classroom violated--
the exploitation of poignant masterful art worthy of any gallery
in the political districts targeted throughout the nation,
rapes the art itself as we ourselves hide from unpleasant facts.

James R. Ellerston
September 25, 2018

With Oak Pews and Blankets

for fifteen years they have laid down their burdens
in this open San Francisco church of the hardwood beds--
bodies and minds sheltered from a hostile world;
in this generous policy allowing, encouraging,
this rest with the Lord.

the lovingly polished oak gleams in tranquil light,
toes protrude from holes in white socks
as the least of these struggle to snooze,
hands clutching the wood pew back as if a parent
reached for in the night, a partner long gone.

homeless are allowed overnight,
are given blankets;
hundreds a day,
no questions asked;
no barriers to entry,
no sign-in sheets or intake forms;
no one ever turned away,
all welcomed with dignity.

two thirds of the church is reserved for them;
they are not kicked-out by those who come to worship;
this is the community of the tired and the poor,
the tempest-tossed with mental health issues;
here the wet, cold, and dirty find a place
offered without judgement in the house of the Lord.

to feel safe is rare in our modern world;
to be welcomed and not be treated like prisoners,
not be victims of laws against the homeless,
to find a place with no chain fences,
with no artificial boulders placed under bridges--
just a welcome pew in a place of beauty,
at St. Boniface since 2004,
known as the Gubbio Project,
but a comforting place to sleep in a hostile world.

in an internet video a mournful blues issues forth
from the magically talented hands
allowed to freely play upon the keys of the piano;
in this church no one pushes the man away,
in an effort to protect David's harp
from the lost sheep of His flock;
there is no criticism of the player in denim,
no deacons' debate about this intruder "not like us";
as the camera fades
people sleep in the valleys of the pews
and for a few hours feel no evil;
the chorus may snore praise in unison;
sometimes the music is beautiful on God's stage.

James R. Ellerston
September 26, 2018

Homecoming 2018

        I.

I met her on the stairway
after the alumni concert;
she was from the class of 1953;
and had come all the way from Alaska;
she had lived there in Fairbanks for decades,
but still was drawn back home here,
to this beloved place from her past and youth;
and she had heard the music of peace and beauty
in the newly renovated auditorium;
she stayed in the home of a grandmother I knew from church,
grandmother of the young man I had known in church choir
since he was an eighth grader and sat next to me as a bass;
such interconnections over distance and time.

        II.

the sidewalk sign downtown had read
"Welcome Central families!"
it should have read
"Welcome members of the Central family."

James R. Ellerston
September 28, 2018

After the Summer of '68

the New York and New Jersey students arriving that fall,
came to Central College with their heads full
of their experiences at Woodstock;
I arrived from an Iowa farm via the University of Kansas,
where the music halls had echoed with the authentic roll
on the timpani in "Irish Tune"
authorized by Grainger himself while teaching at the camp;
my summer it was performed six times weekly
by four bands and two orchestras;
the timpani roll, now missing from the score and lost timpani parts
exists for a lifetime in the memories of music camp attendees;
"Irish Tune" was the camp theme song for decades;
the rest in the score, the G.P., is the location for the roll,
and when performed as silence--
for the teary-eyed listeners who once played there,
sets-off the absence of the roll,
remembered from the past as played *fortissimo*
in thousands of past camp performers' minds.

James R. Ellerston
September 29, 2018

Woodbine Willie (Geoffrey Studdert Kennedy)

the cruel wind had blown the match out three times;
time was running out for the lad--
his blood was running out into the wet mud of the trench.

Willie held the cigarette, a Woodbine,
between the shaking soldier's bluing lips;
his body was in shock, cooling down rapidly.

the Lord is my shepherd...
He maketh me to lie down in green pastures...
I will fear no evil...

a puff of smoke floated into the cold air,
more gray mixed with the smell of cordite;
guns rattled and pounded on.

the wounded inhaled again, lungs gurgled--
the lad tasted the rich tobacco of the Woodbine
and then his head fell to the side.

God's Anglican chaplain gathered up his things,
let go of the cold muddied hand--
and moved seven feet to the next dying man.

Willie fought the breeze to light a match again
all the time gazing into the terrified eyes of a trembling boy
holding the cold soiled hand and started in again.

the boy lasted only to *"beside the still waters"*
in the care of the gentle chaplain, Bible, and smokes,
before his slaughtered life was given its last breath.

purchased at the chaplain's own expense,
the Woodbines with the Bible were his own idea;
he lived in poverty at War's end having held back nothing.

becoming ill himself, the chaplain and poet was sent back home,
to green England from administering morphine in no man's land
with courage in these muddied moments of trench-comforting.

no medal awarded for passing out Woodbines to dying wounded,
but a grateful nation could recognize him for battlefield bravery--
and an empire's king would appoint him as his personal chaplain.

James R. Ellerston
September 29, 2018

Last Car Ride
(from a photo Jessica posted on September 19th)

he was told he was going to the vet;
his tail wagged;
everytime when told he was taking a car ride
he was excited.

normally in the front passenger seat he usually rode,
breathing in fresh air and scents from dash vents;
his entire human family was in the car with him
and he was in the back seat with the child who shared his bed.

cold glass was rolled up in the photo;
his wet nose pressed eagerly against the window
seeing the comforting sights of a familiar journey;
today he just somehow knew he would not be returning home.

today would be his last car ride,
and his journey would be for eternity;
he rode with a doggy smile on his face
feeling the family love that would free him from pain.

he would depart the bodily aches of his last few months
and leave his family's world in grieving tears.

James R. Ellerston
October 3, 2018

Sheila's Horses (in Photographs)

I.

I see a horse's head in a barn,
looking over a half-door;
the sun was on its chestnut coat,
shown upon a white-starred face;
a careful owner, she feeds with care
and trains with rope and halter
each new colt and mare.

They graze days down by the river bank,
spend their time in paddock and field;
not raised for profits,
but the pleasure to her they yield.

II.

These horses upon the lawn
in early morning cast four shadows;
all lying on ground in black
betraying the horses' colors.

Their necks are down,
they graze green grass;
tails are flicking endless numbers of barnyard flies
from shining coated backs.

Beloved by owner,
sheltered in white-roofed red horse barn
between rides and careful feeding loved;
(She lives in a white farmhouse);.

She says "Good morning Trooper, Anne, Isabelle, Midnight;
sending photos' captured beauty across wire and radio wave;
they'll eat their fill of grass
then quench their thirst with the water-filled tank she gave

III.

Two haltered horses are in the barn,
one in red and one in blue--
heads held earnestly over the stall half door;
it's morning, their owner a welcome sight;
bright eyes and lapping tongue say "feed me more".

One horse's blaze shone out
beneath intense eyes' bright gaze,
ears swept back in begging mood;
there are others out on the lawn to graze;
this pair think food from a trough is extra good
this brushed-hair morning in an Iowa shed.

IV.

Midnight, Annie, Trooper, and Isabella on Labor Day,
in a well lit photo dominated with greenness
these four horses stand together;
all their eyes looking toward the camera focal point;
their ears are up attentively listening.

Curved piping forms the gates in front of them
and in back of the animals in the corral;
a galvanized water tank stands to the horses' left;
ground beneath their hooves is muddied from recent rain;
all four heads have halter straps across velvet faces.

Cared-for coats are clean,
shaded beneath a green canopy of trees;
muscles are strongly poised with soft noses near the fence;
green grass growing outside the bars
is mowed too low for nibbling.

James R. Ellerston
June 25, June 28, July 3, September 7, October 3, 2018

dawn celebrated

it was early morning
but I did a boat ride across the calm lake;
I could see my breath behind the windshield;
loons were swimming, calling out;
sun was breaking through the grey clouds
and cold air was chilling the cheekbones;
a great day in northern Minnesota
even though there had been no swimming for several weeks;
a snow was forecast for Tuesday;
fall foliage was colorful,
but soon I fled south from this place.

James R. Ellerston
October 3, 2009 (October 4, 2018)

Easter Sunday Dinner After Church

His adrenalized fist came down on the table
while heirloom Spode English china rattled to attention,
the sterling rolled with cadence in place-set formation.

I had mentioned something about the good works
of the Red Cross around the world;
my father-in-law said he "wouldn't give them a dime".

Internet postings have exposed the Red Cross today,
with excessive overhead, salaries, mis-utilized funds;
in the Pacific theatre he knew this firsthand.

As quartermaster he had gone to the Red Cross station
to pick up cigarettes for his men "in harm's way";
each pack was stamped "Gift of the American People".

A greedy Red Cross (N.C.) behind a money-changers' counter
wanted to assess the soldiers for their smokes;
my father-in-law revolted with acid stomach and sickened gut.

"Sergeant, pull your weapon, hold it on this man!
I will take these cigarettes now.
Do not take your gun down until I am gone."

He had only talked about the war with me three times;
he was usually wearing out typewriters ordering his unit supplies;
he once had jumped into a foxhole with a dead enemy soldier.

His unit built Bailey Bridges for troops to cross waterways,
serving in New Guinea, the Philippines, and Japan;
in rainy darkness he helped build a bridge under fire.

In his engineer's office was a safe
holding locations of where to build bridges
during the upcoming invasion of Japan..

We never debated the merits or politics of nuclear weapons;
in his Christian mind he was always grateful and credited
Truman's use of the A-bombs with saving his life.

James R. Ellerston
October 5, 2018

Prayer for Another Baby

With a technological miracle
I see another fetus in an ultrasound photo
and my hopes and prayers
are seeded in rich soil once again.

I am afraid to put pen to paper,
to write more mere words springing to life--
that this newly germinated dream
might survive its growing season in the womb garden.

Please, this time, no early gush of fluid from her body,
no tears from families' eyes and minds;
a lost baby is remembered in grief forever,
no matter its time of life or cause of anguished death.

With these few months to go, to grow, to develop,
I pray and beg for a healthy baby
from this miracle embryo of implanted hope;
I am feeling love for these new shadows on a data screen.

One sees but dimly the future,
while fighting tears from the past.

James R. Ellerston
October 6, 2018

House Saving Mechanicals

for days now
the rain falls steadily;
plumbing makes gurgling sounds;
I hear the sump pump
growling as it drains,
saving my house,
and keeping it liveable.

James R. Ellerston
October 6, 2018

Encourage Another on Their Journey

I.

I would be with you there if I could;
and I will search for an internet broadcast streaming;
the crowd will be so large at the Marathon,
and you will not be positioned
near the front of the field at the line;
it has only been four weeks since you donated--
gave a kidney to keep another life-traveler going;
the gun will crack and the runners will surge forward
down a Chicago street to compete with self;
with sweaty enthusiasm you will propel your body;
and when your thirty-year-old energy wains
please keep fighting forward
(even if just to walk the course);
in my mind I will keep calling out,
"just one more step, Aaron"
as you struggle with determination on the asphalt,
raising funds for the Kidney Foundation;
as you try to move those cramping legs
and numbing mind as it fogs and oxygen depletes--
within a body that can't clear waste as rapidly
as it once did before you gave hope and life to another--
and no matter your finish ranking
I will still love you
as I always have all these years
since teaching you in elementary school;
I have never forgotten you in my heart,
you were such a talented student.

II.

Rumbling big diesel engines throbbed with impatient power,
yet on the platform, the train conductor had simply stood there,
and had held back his whistle;
I had walked so far in Salzburg that day
with my painful arthritic knees and was depleted;
(this was before both joint replacements);
and Frau commanded me in a teacher-tone,
"just one more step, another one Jim";
everyone else had already boarded, was waiting,
as through the pain I fought my path,
struggled my way so late down the long station platform;
while in his formal uniform he waited expectantly,
holding back breath from the decisive whistle--
it did not sound forth in the noisy *bahnhof*,
as he watched me fight my way past loaded car after car;
"just one step more!" she called-out, again and again;
finally I was there, and the shrill sound trumpeted forth,
my small battle had been won, this day's minor victory;
with this high-pitched applause the train departed the station,
and our student exchange group in Germany
hustled along on its journey with me included;
the train jerked repeatedly on the switching-tracks leaving the station
as it left the "Sound of Music" city behind.

written during a movie in a Pella cinema
James R. Ellerston
October 6, 2018

III.

His forehead sweat droplets of blood
under the spikes of a crown of thorns;
the crowd did not surrender to Him a wide path
as He carried the weighty crossed wood.

Sharp rocks and cobblestones beneath His feet
cut sore cracked dry skin of bared flesh,
(no oil for the convicted and condemned);
of the Man carrying the heavy Cross.

He was carrying the method of His own execution
to the hill outside the city walls called *Golgotha*;
this "place of the skull" utilized for crucifixion of criminals
where many hung for days before death occurred.

Splintered rough wood cut into the flesh of His hands;
the incline through the streets was steep;
legs ached, back was bent; pain was human;
arm muscles were used to giving blessings to others.

The Roman soldier with the lash marching alongside,
offered little positive encouragement as He struggled forward,
bent in broken agony, subject to the cruelty dealt out to this
champion of peace, voice of forgiveness, promiser of eternal life.

Messages of love were shouted out toward this broken person,
but in the loudness of the crowd yelling and screaming--
a person was coming forward out of the swarms of hecklers;
"Take another step, Master, for I shall carry it for you."

Alongside Him the person walked carrying the timbers,
all the way to where nails were spiked into His hands and feet.

James R. Ellerston written in church
October 7, 2018

IV.

halfway through his legs ached with so much pain,
he could barely walk;
he ended up walking 8 of those 26.2 miles,
wanting desperately to be done.

so many times he wanted to stop and call it a day;
this pain was too much; his knees couldn't handle more;
his feet couldn't keep slamming against the ground;
left, right, left, right, ouch, ouch, ouch, ouch!

at one point he couldn't go any further, sat down on the curb;
started doing some futile stretches while runners asked "how he was?";
Rhonda stopped, gave him ibuprofen and biofreeze;
with her and others support he was able to keep going.

he struggled, he grunted, but he went the distance;
with help from his team he somehow finished;
afterwards he could barely stand, barely walk,
and definitely not traverse stairs.

he had successfully finished a marathon
and his team raised over a quarter million dollars
for AIDS Foundation of Chicago; encouraging him along his way
dozens sent audio messages, texts of support, and phone calls.

there is an old 1965 Beach Boys tune that brilliantly says it all--
"help me Rhonda, help, help me Rhonda!"
over and over again it is sung; he onward struggled step after step;
myself, a poor poet, can only write another stanza and type.

words of Brandon Strawn after his first marathon
edited by James R. Ellerston
October 8, 2018

Desire to Communicate with Horses

People have always wanted to talk,
to communicate with animals;
we seek to understand their nonverbal cues,
their body language and sounds, to tell what they want;
we should not expect interaction in written language.

Researchers in Norway taught twenty-three horses
to express their needs using symbol boards;
the research was invalidated when horses were attributed-
after being trained and learning the symbols "to have loved it";
the choices made were dependent on the weather.

To understand the consequences of their choice--
of choosing to have a blanket put on or taken off--
of understanding weather conditions for their own comfort;
the horses still tried to attract attention by vocalizing;
we humans hope to teach teenagers to have "horse sense".

James R. Ellerston
October 7, 2018

October 7th, 2011

wind is blowing.
leaves are falling;
coffee comforts my Facebook
reading and writing;
lots to do today,
music practice
and fall pruning of bushes in the yard;
an ambitious day.

James R. Ellerston
October 8, 2018

Poetry from the Press: Immigration Inquiry

ironically she was imposing in a chair within the witness box,
due to the small size of the toddler, taken from her grandmother;
it was the two-year-old's day in immigration court;
she had been in government custody since July;
Fernanda Jacqueline Davis was taken at the border.

the youngest child that day before the bench awaiting justice
in federal immigration court No. 14,
she is so tender and had been lifted into the chair;
her feet were in small gray sneakers;
the black-robed judge breathed a soft "aww".

perched on the brown leather chair,
with legs too short to dangle,
her feet stuck out from the seat;
fists were stuffed under her knees--
in her brief life, she had already had a long journey.

her caseworker, a big-boned man from the shelter,
had then turned away to go--
and next she had let out a whimper;
in the echoes of the room, it had risen to a thin howl
behind a crumpled face, behind a bursting dam.

before on that confusing day,
her contracted caseworker was the only person
in the big room she had met before;
the judge motioned the caseworker to return to Fernanda's side;
sobbing tears stopped, and the judge asked,
"How old are you? Do you speak Spanish?"

an interpreter bent forward toward the child;
after catching her eye, the question was repeated in Spanish;
Fernanda's pigtails brushed the chair; she stayed silent;
Judge Zagzong peered down in black-rimmed glasses,
and said, "She's nodding her head."

this single afternoon in a New York immigration courtroom
Judge Randa Zagzong would hear from nearly thirty children;
their ages ranged from two through seventeen years;
all were represented by lawyers from Catholic Charities;
Fernanda was No. 26 and was afterward returned to a shelter.

an officious Homeland Security lawyer
did not even look over toward the girl from the government's table;
Judge Zagzong tried to explain the proceedings
to each and every child who sat before her;
the court sat sternly facing the gold-fringed American flag.

Adapted words of Vivian Yea and Miriam Jordan
New York Times of October 8, 2018 as on the Internet
James R. Ellerston
October 9, 10, 2018

Abolution? A Solution

In an atmosphere smelling of candle wax, incense, hypocrisy,
celebrants of the cloth betrayed the trust
of those they were to lead in faith;
camera photos, groping hands, organs of wholesome manhood,
were used by these for cheap thrills and emotional betrayal.

No lengthy trials in court, no defrocking, or demotions occurred;
nothing followed from demented church hierarchy but "Let us pray";
hiding, protecting, not censoring its own, claiming to lose records;
priests are revealed by accusations of people now matured,
men and women now stepping forth, still lost, adrift emotionally.

Abused now are telling their stories with inner shame and outrage,
now that the clock has ticked life painfully away for them in anguish,
mental pain caused by an organization that threatens the unholy--
these very men threaten eternal damnation to others,
but do not believe in it applying to sinners amongst the priesthood.

Betrayed were those in youthful vulnerability taught to believe
in required absolution spoken from the tongues of even immoral --
men of the cloth who betrayed the trust of God's most beautiful,
those in childhood and adolescence--
men who betrayed those they were to lead in faith.

For them the surgical knife should prune the branches of the vine,
clean the vineyard of what is rotten hanging from below the trunk;
it can be done chemically like the British sentence for the convicted,
or with a sharp knife like a skilled technician in any farmyard;
I advocate removing waste with clean cuts below belt and waist.

James R. Ellerston
October 10, 2018

Absolution? A Solution

In an atmosphere smelling of candle wax, incense, hypocrisy,
celebrants of the cloth betrayed the trust
of those they were to lead in faith;
camera photos, groping hands, organs of wholesome manhood,
were used by these for cheap thrills and emotional betrayal.

No lengthy trials in court, no defrocking, or demotions occurred;
nothing followed from demented church hierarchy but "Let us pray";
hiding, protecting, not censoring its own, claiming to lose records;
priests are revealed by accusations of people now matured,
men and women now stepping forth, still lost, adrift emotionally.

Abused now are telling their stories with inner shame and outrage,
now that the clock has ticked life painfully away for them in anguish,
mental pain caused by an organization that threatens the unholy--
these very men threaten eternal damnation to others,
but do not believe in it applying to sinners amongst the priesthood.

Betrayed were those in youthful vulnerability taught to believe
in required absolution spoken from the tongues of even immoral --
men of the cloth who betrayed the trust of God's most beautiful,
those in childhood and adolescence--
men who betrayed those they were to lead in faith.

For them the surgical knife should prune the branches of the vine,
clean the vineyard of what is rotten hanging from below the trunk;
it can be done chemically like the British sentence for the convicted,
or with a sharp knife like a skilled technician in any farmyard;
I advocate removing waste with clean cuts below belt and waist.

James R. Ellerston
October 10, 2018

For Former Student Mike Tuvell

I.

I see you in the pixelated Fred Larson newsprint picture
in a T-shirt standing tall and summer-outdoor tanned,
sunglasses hiding your face a bit, but not your inner pride;
the heavy multi-lugged drum harnessed out front
held proudly with straight back and teen muscled strength;
your sticks in playing position, poised hands astride.

II.

It is the repeated aspects of life,
in the familiarity and comfort they provide;
the past security of sunlit childhood days playing with others,
the variety and challenge of every new event.

Such surprising rhythms are in daily events,
unexpected changes in patterns,
through accident, intervention, or intentional artistry--
creative process and events of natural art on the oldest instrument.

Music makes expectation through repetition-- then mixes it up;
in life, formal cadences keep us going, variation makes interest;
patterns mark our days with rigor, energy, pomp
until followed by the muffled drums behind the funeral bier.

We are able to hear no more the stretched heads,
the resonance of these live vibrating skins
of hide or synthetic wonder material and beaters' contact--
only in listeners' memories will they play on,

III.

I found a piece of your personal history in my basement,
on the flip side of something from my own past saved;
ironically, an article on helping students select instruments;
yours was from the beautiful "Colts' Summer" of your teen youth--
a year you were 16, in the developing years of early manhood.

Drums were a good choice for you;
it was a fit we made together;
I taught music instruments;
luckily you were snared by the sound of sticks on skins
when in three lessons, the trombone died on your fifth grade face.

Fort Dodge Messenger from September 4, 1988
James R. Ellerston
October 11, 2018

For Students: History Writing Must be Verified Again

There must be a search for truth, not blind revisionism;
the young are obligated to hunt, search, and tell history again,
with energy and hormone driven rebellion for independence
during their energetic youthful developing years of life.

An expedition for truth is a solemn obligation, not subversive,
driving the scholar-historian to find that which is correct,
moving poets' pen on paper telling truth using verse as art;
propelling artists' brushes on life's canvas declarations of beauty.

There is no author, no historian without inner self motivation--
all accounts of events must be considered and balanced;
no final version deemed truthful may previously exist;
no ultimate scapegoat may have been found to blame.

Historians must explore the effects of faith and organized religion,
examining viewpoints and opinions taught as sacred text;
presented in original and ancient languages;
often dogma, politics, and national boundaries intervene.

Motivation and documenting action must always be considered;
crematorium operators at Auschwitz wrote their truth under threat,
using the language of ancient Greek written and carefully buried;
doing tasks because the lives of their children were held hostage.

On a bronze plaque next to their entrance portal in Baden-Baden
the Gymnasium Hohenbaden proclaims outside the school,
"Within these wall Leo Wohleb refused to teach Nazi curriculum";
instead were original Greek and Latin productions of plays.

Mankind's tested truths must be retold through drama and art,
not because they are safe, acceptable, or all we have;
but sometimes as an alternative to the teaching of falsehoods;
sometimes the best that might be done for Man in troubled times.

This process is troubled by a long list of --isms in teaching history;
simplification vs. revisionism; accuracy vs. teaching patriotism,
omission vs. inclusion; conservatism vs. liberalism; economics;
there is a problem with accepting comfort zones vs. offending.

Larger issues have surfaced in constructing public monuments;
when is a people a nation vs. a country with a line on a map?
what is the place of politics in art? The governed vs. government?
what place military conquest, the victor, or defeated, vanquished?

Even poet and playwright Shakespeare rewrote many histories;
some colleges do not teach art or world's expressive languages--
humanity has been sacrificed on the bloody altar of STEM,
or how to run a business, not necessarily ethically, but profitably.

Under a million stars, to uphold historical truth--
many must speak independently a single voice in eons' of orbits,
a past loud voice with authority must not forcefully today prevail;
we voyage through a universe on a troubled blue watery sphere.

James R. Ellerston
October 12, 2018

Still Considering Matthew Shepard After Twenty Years

In October 1998 it was hate that killed him
in his twenty-first year dead from prejudice;
it was not the barbs in a thorny crown in the hands of men,
but the splintered wood of a tortuous rail fence that did it.

The boy's crucifixion still causes decent folk to tear;
a child beaten and left in the cold to die;
his parents cremated his body but kept his ashes unburied,
for fear of grave vandalism and desecration.

After twenty years, now this martyr will find a final spot;
his ashes will be interred inside the crypt of a cathedral,
Washington National, near those of Helen Keller, Woodrow Wilson;
it may become a pilgrimage destination.

A dramatic play, "The Laramie Project", about him,
is one of the most performed theatre pieces in the country;
October 26, 2018 his ashes will be place in the *columbarium*,
a private off-limits area, during an Episcopal service.

The cathedral is seat of the Episcopal Church, Shepard's church;
he will be one of two hundred people with remains there;
for the public there may be a plaque for peoples' hands to touch;
fingers being somehow in physical contact with this beautiful victim.

James R. Ellerston
October 13, 2018

Fortune Cookie Truth

we ate at the Chinese buffet, this one
unusual at 4:30 p.m. for freshness and delicious taste;
everything was wonderful, so unusual,
including the message in the fortune cookie.

so many times these small slips disappoint
in their poor syntax or weakness of disappointing thought;
today mine told a universal truth--
my spouse across from me said "put it in a poem".

a poet may be inspired or constantly searching
for that which will pump the pen in hand
with liquid words from the well of thoughts
flowing forth in phrases upon the page.

in life there are people who inspire, move us with humor;
"He deserves paradise, who makes his companions laugh."
good times include love making, cheering a team, holding a baby;
but the greatest of these is laughing with a friend.

James R. Ellerston
October 17, 2018

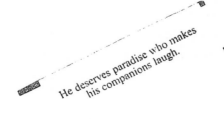

Revised Recipe for Dylan's Dairy Restaurant:
Mix Love, Cancer, A Herd of Milk Cows,

still hunting for a home-cooked country meal
we drive into Cornell, Wisconsin's streets
and spy a corner eatery aptly called
Dylan's Ice Cream and Cheese.

a long refrigerated showcase displays cheddars,
multiple kinds of cheese of different ages fill the shelf;
next to white cheeses with fruits and peppers,
the freezer case displays twenty kinds of homemade ice cream.

on the wall you see Dylan in photos at seventeen years and with leukemia,
and stories that tell of his homegrown wish for "Make A Wish";
it was for a dairy herd to milk morning and night--
for that the Foundation gave him just the first two cows.

town's people donated and held bake sales and raffles;
the herd numbered thirty, then later sixty cows;
an old barn unused for twenty years was eagerly prepared;
milk sold to a dairy was bought back, made into floats, cones, and shakes.

in the early hours his mother rises every morning,
during the pre-dawn light like so many farmers with cows to milk;
in central Wisconsin people have dairy herds;
in the barn in morning and evening she milks the legacy cows.

after cleaning out the barn alleyway, she cleans herself up,
drives to town and makes the restaurant's soup for the day;
behind the shining counter she works so many tasks--
manager, cook, waitperson, busses the dirty dishes.

daily she does her work with purpose while grieving a teen son, years gone;
"Isn't it amazing how strangers can meet--
even though we haven't even met," she wrote in her letter;
this poet had mailed to her an earlier draft of this poem.

in past tense she wrote her son Dylan "seems to have had a way
with connecting so many people together:"
that he "provoked many others to look at themselves,
teaching them things they couldn't figure out on their own".

she felt her son Dylan to be "an extraordinary child,
forced into growing into a man overnight";
now on part of our usual route, we visit Dylan's Dairy;
my wife and I talked with Dylan's mother while she took our orders.

his mother opened the small town's corner restaurant in Dylan's name;
she sells the half-pound burger with cheese and a shake;
it's cooked among "for sale" home-sewn aprons and humorous signs;
a wall-story spread and bald-headed photo are displayed with empathetic fame.

James R. Ellerston
July 27, 2014 and October 17, 2018

Song and Dance in a Gym

only these two dark-haired teen boys did their dance
within the third row of the high school choir;
other singers stood almost still on the risers under a choral shell
in an otherwise staid performance of solemn tunes;
the two boys also sang their low bass parts with zeal.

during some concert songs these two moved in harmony,
in a perfect unison of effort, no exageration,
while the rest of the choir stood almost rigid;
when most singers' faces displayed little emotion--
these boys sang fervently, expressively, with an almost religious feeling.

shoulders rolled, skeletons pulsed, but nothing was sexual, erotic;
just male bodies moving with dancers' ease to the rhythmic pulse--
such syncrony of thoughts they had between them,
their eyes gazing at the other's mirroring of their own movement;
the unison of their unplanned dance was a pleasure to behold.

wearing classic black choir robes with gold-sashes swaying,
they moved in joyous choreography, spiritually united,
feeling good about the music, their young teen bodies so expressive,
and not even aware they were doing something extraordinary,
something so temporary in passing time, so youthful and beautiful.

James R. Ellerston
October 18, 2018

Bridge Over Troubled Waters

a sea of stranded Honduran refugees is on the move;
now at a highway bridge-to-nowhere on the border,
between Guatemala and Mexico;

when you're weary, feeling small,
when tears are in your eyes...
I'm on your side, oh, when times get rough...;

the tearful father holds his child in muscled arms;
families lie down to sleep, not in a welcoming green valley--
but on the hard concrete deck of the critical bridge;

when you're down and out, when you're on the street
when evening falls too hard... when darkness comes...
I will comfort you... I will lay me down.

now marked in history as a humanitarian disaster,
this "Remagen Bridge" is blocked by troops with tear gas;
some crossing the border holding a guide rope in swift waters;

all your dreams are on their way, see how they shine.
Oh, if you need a friend I'm sailing right behind...
like a bridge over troubled water, I will ease your mind.

this desperate international migration is toward a dream
of the golden door opening for a good life
for their children and elderly family members;

your time has come to shine… I will ease your mind…
when darkness comes and pain is all around
like a bridge over troubled water, I will lay me down.

thousands of miles of procession blocked at the request
of a country no longer willing to raise its heralded lamp
beside its ports of entry, now closed to immigrants.

sail on silver… sail on by, your time has come to shine,
all your dreams are on their way…
like a bridge over troubled waters… when darkness comes.

James R. Ellerston
October 20, 2018
lyrics by Paul Simon "Bridge Over Troubled Water"
January 1970
inspired by Reuters photographs of October 19, 2018

October 26, 2018: It Will Come To Pass

they will put your ashes in that place today;
your parents and a grieving world,
will know where you finally are interred;
after twenty years passed of more hatred and fear,
this hallowed space of burial crypt holding famous souls,
a past president, Woodrow Wilson, and blind Helen Keller,
and members of the Episcopal Church like you were,
will let you sleep there forever more.

down beneath those tall stone spires reaching heavenward,
a century's build pointing upward toward God,
who watches our nation's feeble attempts, which still failed you;
yes, left you hanging out in the cold and wind
passing time on a prairie fence all alone,
dust washed from your youthful face,
only beneath your eyes by sorrow's tears,
(not even two convicted thieves provided company beside you).

on a remote bluff outside the city you were secured
to the wood of trees, crossed timbers, these split rails of a fence;
yes, evil left you crucified in the cold outside Laramie to die--
your human search for love and acceptance by hate destroyed;
but now, never forgotten by real people who mourn your loss;
today, good works are now done in your name--
the name of a boy who lived only twenty-one years,
a blond university student, Matthew Shepard.

James R. Ellerston   October 20, 2018

Few Rivers Flow North (Song for the Caravan)

Few rivers in this world flow north to the salty seas,
the Nile, the Rhine, the Red River of the North; these are just a few;
yet these fluid bodies are liquid in their summer journeys' sunlit goals.

This caravan flows toward the United States,
once a hope and dream for all the world--
reaching toward this land of freedom and a better life.

A thousand persons started out, leaving Honduras land;
some from El Salvador too, they crossed into Guatemala's soil,
where they were forced to take a stand.

At the mighty river bridge blocked by the evil hearts of men,
on the Tapachula Bridge above the Suchiate River many slept,
passed the eve with small children in parents' arms sleeping, weeping.

On the bare concrete they laid their hopes and burdens down,
with no food, water, or toilet spent the darkness in the night,
watched over by only humanity's conscience and God's sight.

These migrants do push onward, others joining at their side,
now numbering in the thousands through Mexico they plod,
but a man in a suit, threatens military force to block this human tide.

One gets tweets of terrorists and Middle-Easterners in their midst,
he is sore afraid of people who think differently-- voting with their feet,
on foreign roads they walk, not talk with dollars under legislative domes.

An impotent leader in politics, he screams and rants the floor,
claims this an expedition of the democrats-- "they create mobs, not jobs,"
he threatens our southern neighbors with our aid dollars received no more.

"Only God on high can stop us," they cry out and do believe,
"we're wet, and we still don't have a place to lie for sleep;
forward we march our children in tow; only God on high can stop us now."

What are we to really do, but strum now our guitars and sing,
we can not turn our eyes away blindly from migrants' distant hopes;
let them all flow toward us here, these people in the hopeful stream.

"Only God on high can stop us";
"We are wet, and we still don't have a place to lie for sleep;"
"Only God on high can stop us".

James R. Ellerston
October 22, 2018

Guardian Angels Driving Lanes Among Us

the single small dull red light moved along in rushing traffic,
in front of me in the left lane path--
a lone biker on west-bound I-80 in dark of night.

not the easiest thing to see against rows of lights coming at you,
stabbing my driver's-eyes from the oncoming lanes;
we all had a distance to go, many drove too fast.

yet I observed a beautiful thing, easier could have been left undone,
as over-road truckers their skills did bring to bear--
looking out for another in their multi-lane fighters' ring.

some shadowed the cyclist, lighting up his road,
stayed off behind him, just on purpose, while pulling their load;
keeping their distance, eyes on their mirrors, always watching behind.

when a hastened car approached, not seeing what lay out in front--
they'd blink on their left turn signal, and swerve their load with threat;
slow that hurried car to follow behind, just long enough to see him out ahead.

they were watching out for a fellow driver, helping to keep him safe--
he probably has a reason for speeding westward onward just like me,
for pounding down this pavement under feeble headlights' glare.

more than once I saw a tractor-trailer captain on this ribbon of concrete,
do this simple threatening lane-change thing-- to help keep this man alive,
with safety, care, and the flashing warnings their use of blinkers brought.

James R. Ellerston
October 24, 2018

75th Anniversary "Oklahoma Hello"

inside a darkened and packed performance space,
the wonder of live theater happened again on a high school stage;
the curtain opening on the farmstead scenery made emotions grab,
the first of many times in this drama of dance and song;
on a sparse set with few props ever used or moved,
young teens sang their hearts and souls out
to bring this musical play from Broadway to life again;
from the affirmation of daily wheat-belt life,
by the aisle-entering chaps-clad young man on a beautiful morning;
our entire evening was filled with talent and beauty;
they did the entire dream pantomime by a large troupe of dancers
on a smoke-machine-filled stage;
something really unexpected because of the many rehearsal hours involved;
we, the audience, plowed-through the earthiness of this masterpiece
celebrating life in the Oklahoma Territory before statehood;
we watched young lovers fight their search for a soul mate for life;
I was told how fine the production was by the reaction of my jaded body--
the feeling of my anguished face contorting, wanting to cry and bawl,
my tearing anticipation that this magic world might end;
this bodily reaction let me know inwardly how good it really was--
what I was privileged to view for nearly three hours--
great young people led to be able to do their best,
performing a beloved American masterpiece--
and doing it a level beyond their training and experience
for the enjoyment of themselves, and the hometown audience;
before the show we prayed for the football team away at a game;
I was blessed to be able to get a ticket on a Friday night.

James R. Ellerston
Pella Christian High School presented the show Oct. 25, 26, 27, 2018

Getting The Ashes Home

I watched the Episcopal Bishop convey the cremated ashes,
carry the box down the long aisle during the cathedral service.

I thought of myself driving home from O'hare
with my Mother-in-law's ashes beside me.

They were on the front seat in the sealed copper canister;
she had made a journey up a mountain in Switzerland.

The ashes traveled the overseas airline inside his carry-on duffel--
my father-in-law would not let them be in checked luggage.

Until today Shepard's parents had not let go of their son either,
and had kept the urn of ashes for twenty years without burial.

The Bishop on the altar platform choked up,
paused, fought tears, but continued on with his Homily.

When the first officer arrived at the place on the bluff,
where his battered body had been secured to the timber.

It was a hostile place where wind and dust had blown all night
and cold ruled-- and only tears washed the mud from beneath his eyes.

A small deer was seen lying on the ground beneath him,
had been keeping watch throughout the night..

Until when freed of his Holy obligation by the officer's presence,
the deer looked straight into her eyes before bounding up across the prairie.

The officer said "That was the good Lord,
no doubt in my mind."

The Bishop was stately and serene as he walked
down the long aisle in mourning with the box of Matthew's remains.

I was very nervous driving into the west on the multi-lane expressway,
sun blinding my tear-filled eyes as I drove her ashes in the car alone.

I still remember what unusual music was playing from the dash--
a cassette tape of an accordion concerto with the Auckland Philharmonia.

We had loved the precious persons whose ashes we each conveyed;
from dust to dust, ashes to ashes, these, now safely in His arms of grace.

James R. Ellerston
October 26, 2018

Disguised Hatred is So Political

when grief is faked,
when bigotry is so large
one without scruples
pretends to mourn
a deadly attack on Jews
in sincere prayer
in a synagogue,
debates rage over who and where
to play the consoling role,
and what persons to visit with their hostile beliefs
after seeing the sites of anti-semitic crimes;
this is a tie for thoughtful introspection and self examination;
when anti-Semitic beliefs in the world are inflamed
get an Imam, Rabbi, a Priest, and a minister
and bring all faiths on stage in equal harmony;
it is one's job to bear witness,
to give voice to those who are otherwise abandoned,
victimized and forgotten;
choose not the close and easy--
it is our job to go to great lengths to do so.

James R. Ellerston
October 26, 2018

Alex Craig: Cheerleader for Ending Conflict

and he came to the rumble to make peace between the girls
and he did not break up their battle moving from place to place
and he became a victim of the fight he tried to end
and they fought continuing in an off-campus alley
and more and more curious watched in shame
and the wildfire spread out of control

and they had brought these two from out of state to play ball
and the goons who did this dirty crime did not know his goodness
and they fought with him for no reason
and they beat him down upon the ground using feet to stomp
and the bone of his skull cracked beneath their weight of evil
and he lay there and could not see from the malformed socket

and hatred swept across the recruited field
and in writing some praised those who threw, who caught the ball
and in the hospital bed he could no longer cheer his team on
and many questioned why two thugs had been brought here at all
and the "spokesperson" did not know what the college should do.

and I hold my candle sheltered from this evil wind
and worst nightmares filled with fright again
and they had assaulted him for no real reason
and they may come next for my campus son or daughter
and their "win the game" lack of justice will not satisfy me

James R. Ellerston
October 31, 2018

Friday Afternoon Therapy

This should look like fun;
two saddled horses outside the red barn
waiting patiently, tied up, and secured;
there is a light breeze and unclouded afternoon sun.

A fall day, no jacket needed because it will be warm;
you'll ride with an indulgent husband filled with love;
your satisfied animals are fed hay from mow above;
now it all comes together in life to make a perfect day.

If you're not a horse person, you're missing in a big way,
something to make life worth-living after a week of work;
it's good to be around horses, their soft noses and breath;
God's equine creatures hold your affection, have valued worth.

James R. Ellerston
November 3, 2018

Writers, You Must Do Your Job

I daily do my poet's wordy duty,
my pen scribes upon the mournful page;
It is a powerful weapon,
these typed verses, epigrams, and rhymes;
Even Soviet Stalin feared the words in four line verse--
the effects they would have on citizens' hearts--
and off to the Gulag sent the authors never to be freed;
My goal, not fame or fortune,
but write the powerful words
to bring the greedy politician down.

James R. Ellerston
November 4, 2018

November 5, 2012

Monday morning;
It's a gray day,
not much ambition;
drink a cup of tea,
read an interesting book;
No way!
'cause she left me a honey-do list
(thrust into my tired hands),
and drove my passion away.

James R. Ellerston
revised November 5, 2018

The Humanness of Weeds

One has temptation to say,
"the most human plants are the weeds;
how they cling to man!"
weeds follow him around the world,
springing up wherever he sets his foot!

They crowd his barns and dwellings,
throng his garden;
jostle and override each other
in their strife to be near him;
some are domestic and familiar.

Some, one comes to regard with positive affection--
what a homely human look they have--
motherwort, catnip, plantain, taney, wild mustard;
an integral part of every homestead,
they will draw near your smart new place without waiting long.

Our grass carpets every old door yard;
grass that fringes every walk,
softens every path that knows the feet of children,
or leads to spring or garden, or to the barn;
how kindly one comes to look upon it.

Examine grass with a pocket glass;
see how wonderfully beautiful, exquisite its tiny blossoms;
it loves the human foot;
when the path or place is long disused,
other plants usurp the ground.

One has temptation to say,
"the most human plants are the weeds;
how they cling to man!"
weeds follow him around the world,
springing up wherever he sets his foot!

written by my father, James C. Ellerston c. 1934?
while attending Estherville Junior College
revised by James R. Ellerston
September 1, November 6, 2018

Smokeless Powder in Battle

Use of smokeless powder in battle
stips away what romance and poetry that are left--
like a play without scenery;
it is actors unmasked and half dressed,
all that goes on in the dirty green room.

In the old days the smoke of cannon lay along the grass
for hundreds of feet after the shot had passed;
then it would begin to slowly rise up as if alive,
thicken and drift slowly about, waiting reinforcement
till the whole earth was gray, white, and black with battle.

After only a few successive volleys from artillery
and the curtain fell on the scene--
to rise no more on that act
with no smoke of cannon lying along the ground
for hundreds of feet after the shots had passed.

Now, boom, bang, rip, rattle, tear--
often there are four or five together--
or so close you can't say whether three or five or ten;
there's a sort of rifling sound as if the air
were being torn in two, crosswise and lengthwise at once.

Volume of sound does not seem greater
by the added number of shots;
maybe a single big fieldpiece
is the capacity of the human ear;
until the great guns stop entirely, as they must.

When only the rattle of small arms is heard,
one feels like hissing
the actors of the stage unmasked, and half dressed;
it is like a play without scenery
fought out in the green room.

written by my father, James C. Ellerston c. 1934?
while attending Estherville Junior College
revised by James R. Ellerston
September 1, November 6, 2018

Camping in Colorado

for the campers
one thinks of pleasure, quietness, restfulness,
many beautiful things nature gives us;
a background of snow-capped mountains,
beautiful, tall, sweet smelling pine trees on the slopes,
at the foot a bit of green;
pine cones dot the ground with brown.

the Colorado River is in the valley;
a clear, deep stream makes fishing a joy;
tall thick green grass on both sides of the flow;
it is a good hiding place for ducks;
in a nice clear opening on the south bank
shaded by a few tall pine trees,
one sees a camp pitched.

one has the impression it is morning,
that the campers are preparing breakfast;
a man in the tent opening inquires about the coffee
hanging over the fire on a green stick--
its sweet aroma makes anyone long for breakfast;
the man sits on his knees by the bonfire
frying some fish;
a mother sits beside the tent with waiting children;
they hold plates showing readiness to eat.

with keen observation,
a bowed ridgepole of the tent
shows they have had rain and wind;
wood piled-up by the tent door
suggests the campers are staying a while.

written by my father, James C. Ellerston c. 1934?
while attending Estherville Junior College
revised by James R. Ellerston
September 2, November 6, 2018

The Home My Grandfather Built

My father went out to the well
to get a pail of water,
put the windmill in gear waiting for it to fill;
glancing toward the house for some unknown reason,
he noticed it differently from other mornings.

A large two story square house,
a substantial appearance presenting a beautiful view,
centered in a large green lot on a cement block foundation;
a close-up of two sides
pleased him greatly.

Smoke curled up into the air
drawing attention to the brick chimney;
he liked the west window the best to look out
because he could always see his grandparents' home;
at the top, all four sides of the shingled roof came to a peak.

The sun threw its inviting warm rays on the south side
with its many beautiful colored blooming flowers,
with windows admitting plenty of sunlight,
reminding him of his mother's houseplants in the dining room;
he thought of helping paint the house pearl grey with edging of cherry red.

James C. Ellerston   c. 1934
revised James R. Ellerston
September 2, November 8, 2018

Just A Thought

What good will STEM education
be in a "1984" world
of doublethink?

James R. Ellerston
November 8, 2018

City Tulip Festival Disrupted

movement in the dark Western clouds;
people celebrate the springtime floral growth
with beds of blooming flowers emphasized;
traditional costumes worn from Netherlands heritage.

wail of loud siren for three minute warning agony;
small young-ones run toward shelter in terror;
parents grasp children by the hand moving to safety;
food stand shutters bang down ending evening culinary pleasures.

amazing miracles of modern radar and weather forecasts
tell us exactly where the midwest tornados are on the ground;
tourists get in cars; locals go to houses with broadcast media maps
and seek out protection in cellars below vulnerable frame houses.

late evening cellphones communicate with family, friends, others
and verify that all appear to be safe in their location;
boxes and colors on the state map move slowly eastward distant
to spoil and threaten someone else around their backyard grill.

James R. Ellerston
May 4, 2014

Check out Jim's other books on Amazon.com

(2014) *Poems from Travels in Three Countries: A Collection*

ISBN: 978-1500522476

(2015) *La Grande Guerre: Writings Before and After the Armistice (1918 - 1919)*

ISBN: 978-1505618501

(2015) *Like People, These Are Not Meant to Stand Alone*

ISBN: 978-1511575669

(2015) *Events of Time through Life's History in Poems: 1963 – 2015*

ISBN: 978-1518894503

(2016) *Thoughts, Meditations, and Songs*

ISBN: 978-1523345663

(2016) *The Winds Have Freshened, The Sails Are Full: A Collection*

ISBN: 978-1530579709

(2017) *Newer Thoughts, Older Musings*

ISBN: 978-1544277226

(2018) *Look to the Interests of Others*

ISBN: 978-1981559343

Made in the USA
Middletown, DE
02 February 2019